# Sherlock Holmes
## and the
# Theatre of Death

# Sherlock Holmes
# and the
# Theatre of Death

## Val Andrews

**BREESE
BOOKS
LONDON**

First published in 1997 by
Breese Books Ltd
164 Kensington Park Road, London W11 2ER, England
© Martin Breese Books, 1997

Reprinted February 2000

Front cover photograph of the Empire Theatre, Edinburgh,
is reproduced by kind permission of the MacWilson Collection

ISBN: 0 947533 12 5

Typeset in 11½/14pt Caslon by
Ann Buchan (Typesetters), Middlesex
Printed and bound in Great Britain
by Itchen Printers Limited, Southampton

The better part of a decade has passed since the untimely death of Sigmund Neuberger who was known to the public as the Great Lafayette. He was consumed by those same flames that destroyed most of the backstage area of the Empire Theatre, Edinburgh. It was no ordinary fire and had many bizarre aspects which were investigated by my friend, Mr Sherlock Holmes.

I have, by the way, Holmes's permission, at last, to present the details of this case for your enlightenment and, perhaps, your fascination. Legal constraints have prevented many of the facts of this matter from being made public until now but the recent death of another person involved in the affair has made the publication of some of the more delicate details possible.

John H. Watson, North London, May 1920

# CHAPTER ONE

A t the time of which I will now speak, rather to my surprise I found myself sharing a fishing holiday in Scotland with my friend Mr Sherlock Holmes. The time was early in the April of 1911. The place Taybrook, a village near Perth, and the surprise due to my knowledge that Holmes was singularly uninterested in any sort of country pastime, especially where it entailed the catching and killing of creatures. However, his exile in Sussex, tending his bees, had evidently reached that stage, as it did from time to time, when he craved the company of his only friend.

'My dear Watson, I see that you are contemplating an expedition to Perthshire in pursuit of the poor unfortunate trout.' We were in the study of my north London home and as the table bore the unmistakable preparation for an angling expedition — flies, line and reels — I was not open-mouthed with amazement at this statement.

I said, 'A rather obvious deduction for one of your skill, Holmes, except perhaps for my choice of locality.'

He said, 'Come, Watson, you have a row of books upon angling subjects upon your shelf. I know from experience that you do not allow your domestics into this room so naturally a film of dust has accumulated upon the top edge of each, save for one which has obviously recently been removed, studied and replaced. Its title, *The Trout Streams of Perthshire*. I note also that you plan to complete the expedition before the last week of April.'

Now he had my attention, 'How could you know that?'

He smiled and said, 'Upon the table is your selection of flies for your jaunt.' I agreed and he continued, 'There is no mayfly among your collection. That ephemeral insect with its three tails is irresistible to the largest and finest trout but useless save when the real insect is swarming. This phenomenon occurs only in May, so I need say no more upon the subject, this being the last week in March!'

I felt sure that Holmes must have composed a monograph upon the subject of fishing lures but I did not say so. Instead I showed him the map of the area where I intended to operate; where several tributaries of the Tay provided excellent trout fishing.

Then to my absolute amazement he asked, 'How would you like some company upon your trip, Watson? I need a change of scenery and whilst I do not fish I enjoy communing with nature. I could find a locum apiarist, just as you will have found some aged, partly-retired doctor to look after your patients. Just think, Watson, I can sit there upon the bank, smoking my pipe, observing the birds of the air and beasts of the field whilst you entice the poor misguided trout to take your flies.'

However, our expedition into the wilds of Caledonia was to be delayed by a mild epidemic of scarlet fever and so I did take those mayfly after all. Indeed as I waded in a swift running stream I left Holmes, who sat upon the bank, with strict instructions to watch for the first swarming of the ephemerids. It was already the 11th of May and

I was a little surprised not to have spotted them yet. As it was I caught a few fair-sized trout with the more common imitation dry flies and Holmes would hurry over as each was unhooked and would give me a discourse on each.

Typical of these was, 'Ah yes, Watson, here is an extremely wily customer, more intelligent I think than the average trout.'

Dutifully I would ask, 'Pray how have you come to that conclusion, Holmes?'

He would chuckle and say, 'Why there are three scars upon its mouth, suggesting that he has only partially taken the bait before realizing his mistake and has not, you will note, taken the barb.'

Then suddenly such a post-mortem was interrupted by the arrival of two men in a rowing boat. The man rowing interested us little being obviously just plying his trade as a cab driver would in London. The other man, however — his fare — was standing and peering in our direction with a hawk-like stance. He wore town clothing despite the mildness of the day and the rural Scottish surroundings.

Holmes watched him with interest. 'A legal person, Watson, so I hope you remembered to settle any outstanding accounts before you left London.'

His eyes had narrowed to slits and I knew that his eyesight was keener than my own as he continued, 'Note the marks upon his neck above the collar caused by the long and regular wearing of the advocate's neckband. His briefcase is typical of the lawyer too. Notice how he holds it as if his life depended upon its presence where you or I might have placed it in the bottom of the boat. A man who is anxious to pursue some quest. Let us hope that our holiday is not about to be interrupted.'

Yet I could see that eight years of retirement could not be depended upon to preclude my friend's involvement should he become interested in a particular enigma. It had happened before and there was always a part of Sherlock Holmes which longed for the game to be afoot once more.

As the boat drew level with us where we sat upon the bank the man in the dark grey greatcoat lifted his bowler hat and said, 'By any chance might one of you gentlemen be Mr Sherlock Holmes?'

My friend smiled politely and said, 'I am he and this is my friend and colleague Dr John H. Watson. Might I ask your name, sir?'

The sombrely-clad one said, 'I am Septimus Greyshot of the firm, Luckens, Wild, Luckens and Greyshot, solicitors. Please can you assist me to reach the bank?'

We hauled him up beside us and he gasped and wheezed, then all but collapsed onto a grassy hummock. I suspected a respiratory condition but Holmes probably came nearer in his diagnosis. 'I fear that you have swallowed a flying ant, sir, for I see another adhering to your lower lip. I noticed that you emerged through a cloud of them in your boat. They only fly upon two or three days of each year, and would make a good item for your selection of lures, Watson; seldom used but most effective on those few days.'

The solicitor coughed up the insect and soon recovered. 'I, or should I say, my firm are most desirous to obtain your services, Mr Holmes, upon a certain matter that has occurred in Edinburgh. I tried to trace you through a wire to your colleague Dr Watson and learned that you were somewhere hereabouts. I did quite a little detective work myself in locating you.'

Holmes explained that he was no longer in practice as a consulting detective and had not been for some years but I could see that he was loath to send the solicitor away without hearing him out. I said, 'We are staying at a local inn, sir, the White Hart. Perhaps you would join us there for luncheon and explain further.'

He thanked me, saying, 'I had to forgo my breakfast to journey here from Edinburgh, so I am as hungry as a hunter.'

We climbed into his boat and the good oarsman took the three of us down river to the village. Then we sat in the cool bar-room at a table made from stout Scottish ash and demolished a good steak pie between the three of us. Then over pewter tankards of a local brew our new friend got down to business. I will give the reader the solicitor's story just as we heard it.

'Mr Holmes, Doctor, you may or may not have heard of a theatrically-renowned artiste who appears under the *nom de théâtre* of the Great Lafayette.' (I made one of my only interruptions at this early point in the narrative, telling him that I had myself seen the performer mentioned at a north London music-hall but that I believed that Holmes was rather less interested in vaudeville performances. Holmes waved me to silence so I said little more.)

'Well, his real name was Sigmund Neuberger and he was of German and American origin. In America he had been a protean artiste in vaudeville, after a theatrical apprenticeship as a scene painter. Eventually he enlarged his act until it took in a number of magical illusions which when he combined them with his abilities in the quick-change line made them sensational. Gradually he managed to create a very impressive show involving himself and sometimes as many as a score or more of other performers. Billing himself as the Great Lafayette, he embarked upon a tour of Europe which most recently brought him to these shores.

'The theatrical troupe and production which he headed was of such a scope that he needed to have legal representation which is where my firm and I became involved. He indulged in quite a bit of litigation concerning the content of his performance. To put this into simple terms, other artistes were forever trying to copy his performance in various ways as usually happens when a success is made but, to be perfectly honest, Neuberger would have me take action for him at the drop of a hat, sometimes when it was scarcely justified.

'This tendency to rush into court at the slightest provocation made him far from popular with his fellow professionals. The result of this was that his many eccentricities — and I admit that he was an eccentric — became somewhat exaggerated in variety and vaudeville circles. For example, legend has it that he drilled his assistants like soldiers and forced them to salute him if they should meet in the street. He was certainly a disciplinarian. Then there was the story which would have Lafayette taking advertising posters everywhere and even sticking them on the walls of public wash houses. Here the origin is in his great ability with self-promotion which, however, took more orthodox avenues. But there was one marked form of eccentricity which could hardly need exaggeration because it was truly strange . . .'

He paused and I felt as if I ought to make some remark but Holmes's steely eyes told me not to. So we waited for him to continue. '. . . It concerned his dog, Beauty. About ten years or so ago, in America, Neuberger was given the dog as a gift by his great friend Harry Houdini. It was mongrel dog, with a bit of greyhound in it, the sort that we would call a lurcher. Beauty was not the most attractive of dogs but for some reason Neuberger took to her at once and she very soon became his closest companion and he said that she was his only friend.

'If you went to dinner with him you would be treated to the sight of the dog being seated at the table on a silk cushion and being served by waiters. The house which he recently purchased in London has a plaque over the door which states, "The more I see of men the more I love my dog". On tour the dog had her own rooms at the best hotel, adjoining that of her master's suite. She wore a collar bearing precious stones and her likeness appeared upon all his headed note-paper, contracts and even upon his cheques.

'Neuberger would accept minor discourtesies shown toward himself by persons with whom he came into contact but anyone who, by word or deed, showed any such rudeness to his pet would have broken all contact with him forever. He had a fake pedigree created for his dog, in which she was referred to as an Assyrian Greyhound or some such non-existent breed. The dog even had a few brief appearances in his Great Lafayette act.'

At this point Holmes made his only interruption. He said, 'Mr Greyshot, this is all very interesting but does this Mr Neuberger's obsession with his dog have a bearing on the matter in hand? We find your narrative interesting but I wish you would get to the point!'

He apologized for his long-winded narration and in its continuance he tended to cut a few corners. 'Mr Holmes, he was so besotted with the animal that he was often heard to say that without her his life would be worthless. Imagine, therefore, how worried I became when on Monday of this week he wired me to the effect that his dog had died of apoplexy. He was just starting a second week at the Empire Theatre, Edinburgh, and so I journeyed to Scotland to see if I could be of some help in consoling him. He was quite distraught and insisted that the dog should be buried locally at the Pierpoint cemetery. Of course the local church authorities refused to allow this but I managed to find a way round the problem and offered, upon behalf of my client, to purchase a plot for his own eventual use.

'The authorities eventually agreed to allow the dog to be interred in a vault provided that Neuberger would sign a document to the effect that he promised to make the vault his own last resting place as well. We paid the sixty pounds which they demanded for this vault and hoped that all would be well. Neuberger had the dog embalmed and placed in a glass-topped coffin in readiness for the interment. Doctor Watson, as a theatregoer you will be aware that the variety venues present a twice-nightly system, with the first show at about six and the second one at around eight-thirty. Well, during the six o'clock performance, a Mr Durbar from the funeral directors called round to see Neuberger about Beauty's funeral. He was not from an animal undertakers, mark you, but was a regular funeral director. I do not think his firm would normally have handled an animal's funeral but the Great Lafayette was a big star and Mr Durbar's establishment had the promise of handling his funeral as well when the time came.'

He took a large pocket handkerchief and blew his nose, noisily. 'Little did any of us know that Neuberger, who had already declared that without his dog his life was over, would die within an hour. The second house was nearing its end and the audience had gasped in admiration at the lavish oriental scene which was the setting for the final illusion — the lion's bride. The lion paced its small cage in the palace setting. Beautiful nautch girls gyrated and other assistants appeared as eastern soldiers. There were oriental lanterns and gauze draperies which all added to the splendour of the scene. Neuberger, as the Great Lafayette, in a handsome eastern costume, would have been preparing for his entrance when quite suddenly there appeared a sheet of flame which quickly engulfed the draperies and smoke began to pour from the stage and into the auditorium . . . '

Holmes interrupted. 'I may not be an expert in the vaudeville scene, as both Watson and you have taken pains to make clear, but I am aware that all theatres, legitimate and otherwise, are compelled by law to fit a safety curtain of heavy asbestos to the proscenium, that it may be lowered to isolate such a fire. Was this not operated?'

He replied, 'It was and, as I am sure you know, such a curtain is in three horizontal sections. Two of these dropped into place as planned but the third failed to fall, so that there was a ten-foot gap just above the footlights, through which the acrid smoke soon found the auditorium. The audience behaved well and were dispersed into the street without any problem but backstage the scene was one of a terrible inferno. I promised to get to the point as quickly as possible, so I will just say that ten people perished backstage, including the Great Lafayette, Sigmund Neuberger himself. His body was so badly burned that he was identified only from the costume he was wearing and the huge iron sword which he carried in this particular characterization.'

He paused for so long at this point that we began to think that his narrative was over. At length Holmes, kindly but firmly said, 'Mr Greyshot, I have listened with great attention to your narrative which I have found extremely interesting. This story of a music-hall star and nine others having perished in a terrible fire is a tragic one and the side issue of the man himself being obsessed by a fondness for his dog is intriguing. This man and his canine friend can now be interred together and the episode will be over, will it not, save for some legal complications with which you and your firm will have to deal?'

Greyshot said, 'Alas, sir, that it were that uncomplicated. But you see, Mr Holmes, I believe that there may be some serious misunderstanding regarding the body which is about to be interred. I have reason to believe that the body is not that of Sigmund Neuberger!'

He had our attention now, which he had been in danger of losing. I asked, 'What has put this idea in your mind, sir, as the body is, by your own admission, unrecognizable?'

He replied, 'There were no rings upon his fingers! Lafayette had diamond rings, of immense value, upon almost every finger of each hand.'

Holmes said, 'Perhaps he had removed them and left them in his dressing room or in some place of safety?'

Greyshot quickly retorted, 'If he did it would be the first time that he had ever appeared on stage without them that I or any surviving member of his staff could remember. I did look in the dressing room — though with great difficulty because it was badly gutted. There was no sign of the rings which I am sure you will agree would have survived the fire.'

Holmes nodded and said, 'Quite apart from the tragedy of your client's death, his estate, for which you are responsible, will be the poorer for this loss. Were the rings insured?'

He replied, 'Yes, but the circumstances may make it difficult for the estate to make a claim. I felt honour-bound to mention the missing rings to the police but the inspector involved seems singularly unaffected by my views. He is sure that I am mistaken and that the body is that of Neuberger. He is convinced that the death is through misadventure and therefore does not even require an inquest. I am helpless to do more than I have done and I implore you, Mr Holmes, to accompany me to Edinburgh. The authorities may listen to you. Time is not on our side because the funeral is set for Saturday which gives us only three days in which to act.'

Holmes emptied his tankard slowly and recharged his pipe with Scottish mixture with irritating precision. He said, 'In London I can buy this Scottish mixture from most tobacconists but here in Scotland it seems to be rarely available. Yes, I will accompany you to Edinburgh, Greyshot. Much as I hate to forgo my fishing holiday there are aspects of this affair that intrigue me. Watson, I suppose a few days away from the river will be out of the question for you?'

Hastily I said, 'My dear Holmes, you know I would be happy to go with you to Edinburgh. Why, I haven't seen Arthur's Seat for years, since my student days.'

And so within the hour we had entrained for Edinburgh. I wondered if what lay ahead would be another episode to remember or merely an interrupted fishing expedition.

On the train journey from Perth to Edinburgh I was, as so often in the past, pressed into service to take notes for Holmes concerning salient points as he interrogated Greyshot. For now the time had passed for the solicitor to narrate; now he was questioned thoroughly on a number of matters which at the time at least seemed to Holmes to be important. 'Mr Greyshot, I realize that the fire on the stage started very quickly but, with the regulations enforced by most first-class theatres, I am surprised and, of course, dismayed to hear that the death toll was so heavy. Surely there were means of egress for the people backstage?'

Greyshot said, 'There certainly were and they conformed to regulations, but those who were cut off by the flames, including Neuberger, had evidently relied upon a pass door which would have led them to the comparative safety of the auditorium. Those who escaped had taken the opposite means of exit through the stage door and adjacent fire exits.'

Holmes showed interest. 'You mean the pass door was locked?'

He nodded. 'That is what transpired.'

I dared to ask, 'Was this not rather unusual?'

'Unusual and illegal but I would rather that too much was not made of this.'

Holmes said sternly, 'Ten people lost their lives as a

consequence of that door being locked, Mr Greyshot. How can I or anyone else be expected to make little of it?'

The solicitor looked sheepish as he said, 'Apart from the legal aspect there is the insurance to be considered. If the assurance company involved hear of this there may be some difficulty in getting them to pay.'

Holmes snapped, 'But this surely will only reflect badly upon the theatre management and will not affect your client . . . will it not?'

His shrewd eyes held Greyshot's gaze, and the solicitor's voice all but shook as he said, 'Mr Holmes, the door was locked at Neuberger's express instructions.'

There was an atmosphere and silence that you could have cut with a knife. Eventually Holmes said, 'Sir, what possible reason could there have been for your client to have issued instructions for such an important means of safe exit to be immobilized?'

Rather guiltily Greyshot said, 'To preserve his secrets, Mr Holmes. He was forever being spied upon by fellow illusionists and even by members of the public who were simply curious. The journalistic fraternity were also notorious for trying to learn his methods that they might publish them for their readers' benefit.'

Holmes was genuinely surprised. 'You mean to tell me that a stage magician's secrets are of such public interest? I am more than surprised.'

I was surprised too, though not to the extent of my friend. In my student days I had seen the wonders of Maskelyne and Devant and even in my middle age had retained an interest in such practitioners of the stage illusionist's art. As already mentioned, I had seen a performance by the Great Lafayette and his company a short while earlier.

I said, 'People are indeed puzzled by such things, Holmes, and some are determined to learn how it is all done. Mr Neuberger's performance as I witnessed it, however, seemed to have a rather wider appeal, presenting colour, music, spectacle and of course wild animals that appeared and disappeared with amazing facility. Probably, Mr Greyshot, you have witnessed the performance many times and could give Holmes a better idea of its style and content than I could?'

Holmes indicated that this might be useful and Greyshot gave a very good description of a typical performance by the Great Lafayette.

· 'Well, the curtain went up on a stage full of properties and Lafayette started in an orthodox manner, producing pigeons, ducks and his dog. Then this led up to a very unusual illusion in which Lafayette, as a sculptor, created the figure of a girl from lumps of clay. The figure came to life and posed amidst multi-coloured fountains which suddenly materialized. Now Mr Holmes, Dr Watson, what I have so far described might be typical of any great illusionist but from that point onward the performance would go into realms of fantasy. Still in the persona of an artist he would take an Arabian assistant and transform his costume into an ever-changing parade of characters, everything from Lloyd George to the Tsar of Russia. Then he would walk offstage and instantly — instantly, mark you — the Arabian would remove his outer costume to reveal himself as Lafayette!'

Holmes interrupted. 'You suggest that he did this without recourse to a stage double?'

Greyshot confirmed that this was a fact. 'Yes, sir, and it happened just as I have described. You see he always told me that there were only seven principles in the illusionist's armoury but that he had discovered an eighth! Take the final offering, the lion's bride, the scene that was being enacted when the fire started. It took the form of a playlet and, without bothering you with the full details, the plot dealt with a princess who was about to be thrown into a lion's cage. The audience saw her being trussed up ready to be sacrificed, whilst the very real, full-maned lion paced the small cage. Lafayette, disguised as an Arab warrior and playing her lover, entered on his wonderful black horse. As the assistants made to thrust the princess into the cage, Lafayette leapt into the fray and attacked the lion. The animal reared up on its hind legs and removed its own headpiece to reveal that it was in fact the Great Lafayette — yet another of his miraculous transpositions. However, on the fateful night that point in the piece had not quite been reached.'

Holmes considered what he had heard and then said, 'Mr Greyshot, I do hope that you are not going to suggest to me that Neuberger had some sort of supernatural powers?'

He replied, 'No, sir, I am just stating the effect that his performances had upon his audience, without though trying to explain it myself . . . how can one person change places with another, however clever the magician may be?'

By this time I had filled my angling almanac with notes and was rummaging in my pockets for fresh writing paper. Holmes had knocked out his pipe and was recharging it as he said, 'I would rather we spent the rest of the journey discussing useful facts rather than discussing fables. Tell me more of the fire itself; you say that it is thought to have started by curtains catching fire from a naked flame on a hanging ornamental lamp? I am not myself as familiar with the bylaws governing such things, as I am sure you are yourself, Greyshot, but it occurs to me that those fabrics must have been treated to prevent such an occurrence. Presumably the painted scenery must have likewise have been prepared to resist fire?'

Greyshot agreed, saying, 'Everything was just as it should have been in that respect, Mr Holmes.'

My friend looked thoughtful and said, 'And yet the stage became an inferno within less than a minute. Ah well, doubtless we shall learn more from an examination of the tragic scene.'

# CHAPTER TWO

I t would normally have been a pleasure for me to be in Auld Reekie again for the first time in many years had it not been for the tragic circumstances of our visit. At Edinburgh Station, Greyshot hailed the first cab on the rank, producing a sharp intake of breath from Holmes who would, of course, have taken the third.

It was but a short ride to the shell of the Empire Theatre, and we passed my old seat of learning as we gained Nicolson Street. As we descended from the cab, we noted that the theatre façade still bore publicity for the Great Lafayette. Many idlers and passers-by would have investigated the place more closely were it not for a considerable police presence. We noticed a big mauve Mercedes motor car standing right outside the theatre entrance. It had large capital L's emblazoned on its doors, together with a likeness of the dog, Beauty. 'It has been there since the tragic night,' said Greyshot. But Holmes showed little interest in it, peering ahead through the guarded theatre lobby like a golden eagle searching for a stray lamb. There was, however, nothing sheepish about Inspector Dougal McCloud who greeted us with Caledonian crustiness.

The inspector was short for a policeman, only a shade over the official minimum height. He had a shaggy head of greying hair and a moustache to match; he spoke with a husky voice in a Glaswegian accent, though without the difficulty with the letter T experienced by many denizens of that great Scottish city. 'I ken ye are Sherlock Holmes, no need for introductions, I've heard all about ye from my friend Inspector Lestrade of Scotland Yard. He tells me that you are an interfering fellow but canny!'

Holmes smiled, bowed and said, 'Well in that case, Inspector, I will just introduce you to my friend and colleague . . .'

But the inspector cut him short. 'Oh aye, it'll be Dr Watson. Man, I've read your scribblings in *The Strand*, and I'm bound to tell you that they are blather for the most part. I've no idea why Greyshot has brought the pair of you here, for there appears to be no crime involved.'

Holmes asked, 'Why then are you devoting time to it yourself, Inspector, when you have been so busy with a case involving illegally-slaughtered highland cattle?'

The inspector started. 'How did ye know about Campbell's bulls? Man, some busybody must have told you.'

Holmes smiled. 'I hardly needed to be told my dear McCloud, for the mud upon your boots is of the farmyard variety, as are the particles of hay upon your jacket, whilst upon your sleeve you still bear traces of bloodstained hairs from a particular breed of cattle found mostly in the Scottish highlands. Notice, Watson, the slight tendency to curl which each hair has. The blood shows that the wounds involved were inflicted two or three days ago. I would look for a tall man, left-handed and —'

McCloud all but lost his temper, 'Stop your blather, man! The wrongdoer has been apprehended and is in Glasgow gaol the now! I came here to investigate in case arson was involved but I very much doubt it given the circumstances. You and your nosy friend are welcome to look around, as Greyshot wishes it, but don't get in my way or interfere with police business whatever you do.'

Rather to my surprise Holmes accepted all this rudeness with great dignity and charm, simply saying, 'Remember me to Lestrade when you see him, my dear Inspector. Now, Watson and I will take advantage of your kind invitation to inspect the scene of the tragedy. Come, Watson, we must not take up any more of the inspector's valuable time.'

These niceties completed, the inspector grudgingly allowed his assistant, a Sergeant Ferguson, to show us around the ruined theatre. He led us through the grimy but smoke-damaged auditorium where a number of people were sitting in the seats, close to the orchestra pit which had survived the fire. The sergeant told us that they were all 'Interested parties that the inspector still wishes to interview; surviving members of Lafayette's company, stage hands and other involved parties.' He led us between some columns towards the proscenium and up a number of steps which were between the stage and the lowest of the boxes. From the top of the few steps we turned to our left and he led us through a pass door.

Holmes enquired, 'This would be the infamous door which was locked when it should have been a safety exit?'

The sergeant nodded. 'There are two or three other such doors but at least one of the others was locked and another blocked off by some scenery.'

Holmes mused, 'All this to preserve an illusionist's secrets — a terrible price to pay.'

The sergeant grunted. 'Neuberger himself was responsible for breaking all the safety rules and himself paid the price along with the others.'

We examined the door and then Holmes enquired as to where the bodies of the victims were being kept. The policeman said, 'Well, some of them are with local undertakers; others have been sent home to their grieving families. There seemed little point in keeping them.'

Holmes asked, 'What of Neuberger himself? Where is his body? I would like to see it, and I feel sure that it has not been sent to America!'

Ferguson replied, 'No, sir, to Glasgow to an undertaker there.'

I asked, 'Why not to a local undertaker; dare I ask?'

The sergeant shrugged. 'I do not know but perhaps the inspector does.'

But it was Greyshot who told us why the body had been sent away, when we spoke with him following a cursory examination of the ruined stage area. This was sad to see and it looked like a scene from Dante's *Inferno* after the flames had been quenched. It was back in the auditorium that the solicitor told us, 'Something to do with his will . . . had to be a certain type of undertaker.'

He seemed a little vague but Holmes was suddenly alert. 'Is it possible to have the body returned, untouched, here to Edinburgh?'

The inspector snapped, 'Man, I knew I should not have allowed you to interfere. What possible point would there be in having the body returned? He was burnt to a frazzle, ye ken, only identifiable by the shreds of the costume he was wearing and the sword he carried in his hand.'

Holmes was firm. 'I would still like to examine the body.'

The inspector breathed hard. 'I canna stop you. It is between you and Greyshot here.'

The solicitor told us that the body had been sent to Glasgow by an early morning train. The undertaker proved to be an old-fashioned firm, without a telephone. Holmes sent a telegram:

PLEASE RETURN NEUBERGER BODY INTACT JUST AS RECEIVED
STOP SHERLOCK HOLMES

The wire which arrived back within two hours read:

RETURNING NEUBERGER CADAVER STOP YOUR WIRE TOO LATE
STOP HAVE ALREADY PROCESSED IT STOP CANNON AND
CARSTAIRS

Holmes laughed bitterly, 'Such an enterprising and prompt service friends Cannon and Carstairs operate. However, we must do our best even if embalming keeps secrets from us.'

We took a cab to the station where we impatiently awaited the train from Glasgow. It was not that the express was late but just that we were early in case it should arrive ahead of its scheduled time. When at last it pulled in amidst smoke and the grinding of wheels upon steel tracks, we were already precisely in place on the platform to be in line with the guard's van. As the van door slid sideways Holmes was eager to see that which he needed; a coffin, or at least a packing case with the look of a box that might contain a grisly sarcophagus. Alas, no such sight greeted our eyes. The van appeared to contain only a basket with live pigeons, a large crate with a furnishing company's trademark stencilled upon it, a lawn mower with a label tied to its handle and with a number of assorted packages.

When Holmes demanded to know what had happened to the body of one Sigmund Neuberger, which we were expecting, the guard handed him a small wooden box, saying, 'You will have to sign for the poor gentleman. I wouldn't like to have this done to me when I'm gone. I don't hold with these new-fangled ideas, not fitting to burn the dead, I say!'

As if in a trance, we let Greyshot sign for the crated urn of Neuberger's ashes. We stood there for what seemed an age before any of us spoke. Then at last, just as the train was being prepared for its return to Glasgow, Holmes said, 'Upon my word, he has been cremated! There is to my knowledge no crematorium in Edinburgh, which explains why the body had to go to Glasgow. You had no inkling of any of this, Greyshot?'

The legal man was greatly embarrassed. 'None at all. I will have to look again at his will. My apologies, Mr Holmes, there has been a slip-up entirely through my own carelessness.'

We took rooms at the Royal Caledonian Hotel, the very establishment at which Lafayette, himself, had been staying. The staff were easy to extract information from concerning Neuberger but mostly it was about his eccentricities regarding his dog. The maids would be full of stories of how they had to make the dog's special bed each morning, changing the silk monogrammed sheets. The waiters would be more than willing to discuss the serving of the many courses of the dog's dinner. One of them said, 'Aye, they tell me the wee beastie died of the apoplexy but 'tis my belief that she was pampered to death, ye ken?'

We took a light lunch of cold fowl washed down with a tolerable hock as we tried to calm the all-but-frantic Greyshot. He had done some preliminary reading of Neuberger's will and said, in rather an animated fashion, 'I not only slipped up on the point regarding the cremation but I helped to identify the body as being that of Neuberger.'

Holmes calmed him, yet I could tell that he was seeking more information as he did so. 'Come, my dear fellow, you had no reason to believe that this body, wearing remnants of the Great Lafayette costume and bearing his sword was anyone other than Neuberger. But regarding the missing diamond rings, it occurs to me that these might be missing not through theft but because they are still upon the fingers of the real Neuberger, as yet undiscovered. Let us return to the theatre and see what else we can discover. I must, in any case, give the ashes into the hands of the good Inspector McCloud.' There was only the faintest trace of irony in his voice.

We walked back to the theatre with Holmes insisting upon treating us to his discourse upon the sights of Edinburgh, with which I was the more familiar. But I knew that, as ever, there was a method in his madness. For I knew him well enough to know that he was mentally framing exactly what he needed to do and say, back at the Empire.

He had insisted upon opening the crate so that the urn containing the ashes was more portable and he carried it himself in a raffia shopping bag which was a part of my fishing equipment. Greyshot watched with agony as he swung the bag in his hand.

Inspector McCloud was not entirely delighted at our

reappearance, backstage at the Empire. He snapped, 'Well, Holmes, what have got for us in your wee bag? Some clues to the tragedy? Such I call it, for there is no mystery.'

Holmes brought the urn forth from the bag and said, 'But there is a question of uncertainty, my dear McCloud. I must hand over to you the ashes purporting to be those of Sigmund Neuberger or the Great Lafayette, whichever you prefer to call him.'

The inspector took the urn and said, 'So, he has been cremated, well that makes it all rather more simple. It is not as if we have his body to worry about any more.'

Holmes snapped, 'Sir, the body might have told me something that I might wish to learn. These ashes will tell me nothing. I expected a body in return for my wire.'

McCloud was almost apoplectic. 'You interfered with my case and wired for the body to be sent to you? Man, ye had no right to do that. Fortunately I have no further use for the body, cremated or otherwise!'

Sherlock Holmes remained icily calm as he dealt with the irritable Scottish detective inspector. His voice took on a firm tone, whilst he was still extremely polite. He said, 'Firstly, sir, if you had, as you state, no further need for the body then why should my claiming of these ashes on behalf of Mr Greyshot, who is my client, concern you at all? But, my dear McCloud, before you answer let me add that you should still be seeking Neuberger's body.'

McCloud's eyes dilated as he said angrily, 'Man, are ye daft, for I hold his remains in my hand!'

Holmes said, 'Eventually when you find the actual body of the Great Lafayette you will realize the sanity of my statement; that is *if* you find it!'

The inspector handed the urn to an underling as, with a gesture of dismissal, he walked away from us. After a certain amount of experiment we managed to find three of the once-splendid, plush tip-up seats which we could occupy. A row or so behind us, a row of similarly functional seats was still occupied by a number of persons who doubtless awaited McCloud's pleasure to be questioned. But since we had last seen them a couple of fresh faces had appeared in their midst. They were those of a white-haired man with a matching walrus moustache, wearing an expensive-looking greatcoat with a velvet trim to its collar, which was turned up against the draught. The other was that of a younger man with dark suit and holding a document case. At a guess, I would have said that he was a servant of the older man. Greyshot recognized them at once and waved a hand, as if in salutation. The distinguished-looking man nodded curtly to him and muttered something to the police constable, who appeared to be in charge of the group. Evidently having been given a leave of absence, he made for where we were seated, motioning the other man to follow.

We arose from our seats as Greyshot introduced us. 'Sir Edward Moss, allow me to present Mr Sherlock Holmes and Dr Watson.' He continued, 'This gentleman is the owner and director of the great theatre chain which bears his name, and to which this once splendid Empire belongs.'

We shook hands and Sir Edward spoke with the keen, clipped speech of one who is used to having his own way. He said, 'My dear sirs, I know you both by reputation and can assure you of my generosity in the matter of fees if you can throw some light upon the tragedy which has some rather mysterious aspects.'

Holmes replied sharply. 'Sir Edward, I am retired from professional work but when in the midst of it I always operated a fixed set of charges, which I never varied save where I omitted them altogether. I was on a fishing holiday, and came here at the request of Neuberger's solicitor, Mr Greyshot. But do tell me of the mysterious circumstances to which you refer.'

The theatre magnate was obviously not used to being put in his place and coughed irritably. Then he brushed his moustache with his fingers and said, 'Well, the outbreak of the fire itself is mysterious. This is a brand-new theatre, designed for me by my architect Mr Matcham, and only very recently opened. It incorporated every possible safety device, against such a tragic occurrence, to make it safe for patrons and players alike.

'A safety curtain, of the very finest make and design, did not operate smoothly, and fire-proofing, of all backstage properties and constructions, entirely failed to be effective. A backstage safety regime was completely ineffective and exits and entrances remained blocked. Of course Lafayette had a lot of elaborate properties and curtains of his own but all of them were checked regularly regarding fire safety when he played our other theatres, always passing all tests. I am told that the fire was caused by his hanging lantern catching a piece of curtain; but I doubt this, that drapery was fire-proofed just like the others, and the fire must have taken hold with incredible speed.'

Holmes nodded. 'I had doubts too, when told of how the fire started. I have tried to investigate, as best I could, but have not been encouraged in my activities by Inspector McCloud. Not that I can blame him, of course, for not wanting his official investigations tampered with; the police are pretty universal in this respect. But there is another, perhaps more pressing, aspect to it all in that I believe the body sent to Glasgow for cremation was not that of Sigmund Neuberger.'

'What?' Sir Edward groped for a monocle and screwed it into his left eye as if increased vision might clarify this matter. He spluttered, 'Then whose body is it, and where is Neuberger's?'

Holmes characteristically took out his pipe and started to fill it with the Scottish mixture. We had to wait until he had charged the pipe and produced an acrid blue smoke through the application of a lit vesta, before he replied. 'I cannot, Sir Edward, immediately answer either question. Given more opportunity to investigate, I might answer the first. Do you have any photographs of the entire Lafayette touring company?'

Sir Edward clicked his fingers and his servant, who appeared to be his secretary, smartly removed a folio from the document case and handed it to Holmes. The detective opened it, to reveal about a dozen photographs, uniform in size, about eight inches by ten, which appeared to be of the kind intended for display outside of theatres.

Holmes spread some of the pictures for inspection, asking, 'May I retain these for a day or two?'

Moss shrugged and said, 'You may keep them, for obviously I have no further use for them!'

Greyshot, Holmes and I peered at the pictures as Holmes spread them out. He said, 'One of these may give some clue to an aspect that has already crossed my mind. Rest assured, Sir Edward, I will keep you informed as to my progress, subject to the approval of Mr Greyshot.'

Moss grunted as he prepared to depart. 'Be sure that McCloud will not hamper your enquiries further once I have had a word with him.' He nodded and he and his secretary returned to that group from which they had earlier emerged.

Holmes picked out a photograph for further and more detailed special examination. It was not, as were most of the others, a picture of some aspect of the Lafayette presentation. Rather it was a group of persons standing upon the steps of the front of a theatre. There were five men forming a front row, with some half-a-dozen women peering between the spaces between their heads. These women were evidently standing upon a shallow step which raised them in height. To one side stood two people, very much smaller than any others in the picture.

As he gazed at the picture Holmes said quietly, 'Watson, you have just had a good lesson in how to deal with two pompous persons at once, by setting one upon the other. Who are the very small people at the side of the picture, Greyshot?'

The solicitor replied, 'Alice Dale and Joseph Coats, both of whom unfortunately perished in the fire. Alice was valuable to Neuberger on account of her diminutive height and petite build. In an animal costume she impersonated a teddy bear and, being something of an acrobat, she made this impersonation popular with younger members of the audience. Neuberger became anxious that she had no understudy, so a dwarf, Joseph Coats, was employed to understudy her.'

Holmes took his lens to the picture, 'He is a midget rather than a dwarf, Greyshot — see how well proportioned he was. He directed his gaze at the others in the group. 'This is the entire Lafayette company, I understood there were more people involved?

Greyshot replied, 'The dozen or so depicted are the principals, a troupe that remained mainly unchanged. There were of course various supernumeraries and girl dancers who were frequently being changed.'

Holmes nodded and passed the picture to me. 'What do you make of the picture, Watson?'

I looked at it keenly and then said, 'Well, aside from the numbers of men and women and the two small people, I have little to add except that obviously Neuberger is the central figure in the front row, with the dog at his feet. I see little else of any moment.'

Sherlock Holmes pointed with the handle of his lens to the central figure. 'Neuberger appears to be a man of average height, almost the same in fact as the man who stands on his right. The other three men are taller. Who is the man on his right?'

Greyshot said, 'Charles Richards, principal assistant, also missing and presumed to have perished in the flames.'

Holmes nodded wisely and having asked the identity of several of the other persons in the group he closed the folio, having returned the pictures to it. He handed the folio to me for safe keeping and said, 'Come, let us visit the main scene of the tragedy again.'

Inspector McCloud greeted us with mock charm, having evidently received some kind of message from Sir Edward Moss. He grinned hugely and said with ingratiating sarcasm,

'Oh, Mr Holmes, how nice of you to grace us with your brilliant presence again. Tell me, have you made any great deductions yet concerning our little problem?'

Holmes smiled indulgently and said, 'Nothing much as yet, Inspector, except that I believe I can identify the body that was cremated in error for that of Sigmund Neuberger.'

The inspector started, and his expression changed to one of concerned disbelief. 'What do ye mean, man? Explain yourself at once!'

Holmes replied calmly, 'It transpires that he who was cremated was in fact one Charles Richards, right-hand man and confidante to the Great Lafayette.'

Something of the confident tone with which Holmes spoke made McCloud quieter in his scepticism, 'How do you arrive at that conclusion, man?'

Holmes removed the photograph that we had been studying and showed it to McCloud. He pointed out the similarity in the height of the two men, saying, 'The other men are all above average height.'

The inspector looked uncomprehendingly at Holmes, saying, 'There are several male bodies impossible to identify.'

Holmes almost snapped, 'Check the height of each male cadaver and I'll wager they will all be five feet nine or more. Neuberger was not tall and neither was Richards. Dressed in an identical costume and holding his sword it could have been easy to make this mistake where the features could not be identified.'

The police inspector clearly still did not fully understand and neither, I confess, did I. But Holmes enlarged upon his theory. 'Greyshot, when you described some of the wonders performed by the Great Lafayette, I realized that despite your assurance that no identical twin was involved there, none the less, there must have been some kind of double employed. A man cannot be in two places at once. I have little faith in the supernatural, so Neuberger had to have a trusted employee at least near to himself in height and build. So, given the sword and shreds of burned costume as the only forms of identification, I believe my theory deserves your consideration. Had the body not been cremated, I believe that I could have found other things to bear out my belief. Also we have the fact of the diamond rings having been missing from the so-called Neuberger cadaver.'

McCloud brightened as he said, 'Anyway, whilst you have been theorizing I have made a discovery of real importance. Follow me and you will see a sight that might give you a horrible surprise.'

We followed him backstage where he pointed to a charred pile of rubble in a corner. Our eyes following his dramatically pointed finger. We saw amongst the charred debris what appeared to be a human hand.

I gasped, 'How did you happen to miss finding this earlier?'

He replied, 'It showed up when we started to shift some of this rubble, it having lain there hidden. I imagine some poor fellow got his hand caught up in something and he burned to death. His hand protected by some masonry.'

Holmes looked sceptical, 'I very much doubt it, Inspector.'

McCloud rounded on him fiercely, 'What makes you say that?'

Holmes replied, 'Because it is an imitation, doubtless made for theatrical purposes.'

McCloud was sarcastic, 'You can tell that can you by looking at it from six feet away?'

Holmes retorted, 'I have excellent eyesight, especially for one of my years, Inspector, and I can — even from this vantage point — see newsprint exposed where the heat has raised the paint at the wrist. It is fashioned from papier mâché, formed by the repeated layers of torn newspaper.'

McCloud looked startled for a moment but as the full truth of it all was proven by his actual handling of the grisly object he tried to make us believe that he had known that truth all along. He said, 'Just a little test for you, Holmes, but you are sharper than I supposed.'

He was, however from this point onward, a trace less arrogant in his attitude. He even agreed that Holmes might question some of those whose patience was fast becoming exhausted in the auditorium. First, however, my friend decided to make a more thorough examination of the fire scene itself.

The burned remains of the lantern which was supposed to have started the fire still hung over the centre of the stage. Holmes stood upon a box to examine it more closely. Then he said, 'McCloud, may I suggest that you examine the remains of the lantern more closely. You will find that it is of the electrical variety, though somewhat low powered. I understood that an actual flame lantern had been involved.'

McCloud motioned to a constable to see to the lantern. He said, 'I wondered about that, an open flame would have been asking for trouble.'

Toward the back wall of the stage, now in view through

the collapse of the burned drapes, stood the twisted heap of metal bars and steel sheets burned nearly black which had once been the lion's cage. We were told that the poor roasted beast had been removed from this wreckage.

We eventually returned to the auditorium, having examined a few other pieces of burned debris. We were informed that Sir Edward Moss had decided to take himself off, permission or no, but the rest of the weary-looking persons involved still sat there.

# CHAPTER THREE

Most of the fatal casualties of the tragedy had been among the principals of the company of the Great Lafayette. In fact, of the regular touring performers only an attractive blonde lady and a tall, swarthy man remained. There were of course others involved who sat with them; the theatre manager for instance and the musical director, and another who was a journalist working for the *Edinburgh Informer* — a daily newspaper. Holmes introduced himself to each of them, passing along the space which conveniently existed before that block of stalls in which they sat. Then he started his interrogations with the blonde lady who rejoiced in the stage name of Louise Latour. She admitted that it was a *nom de théâtre*, telling us that she was actually Lilly Davis, 'But Louise Latour has a continental ring to it, don'cha think, dearie?'

She spoke with an east London accent which seemed to lay a little short of her having been born within the sound of Bow Bells. Holmes got the place of her birth with extreme accuracy, 'You originate from Greenwich, Miss Latour?'

She was surprised at his words, 'Blimey, I come from Kent really; but I was born and raised in Greenwich until I was about eight years old. Then we decided to stay in

Edenbridge where we went each summer, 'opping!'

Holmes nodded gravely, 'That would account for the slight modification of your basic south London accent. Those born in Greenwich have a version of this style of speech which has been affected to some extent by the seafarers who mix with the local populace. But I admit that I missed out on the Kentish softening. You worked as a performer with the Lafayette company did you not?'

She nodded, her rather harsh expression, made mask-like with cosmetics being softened at once when she smiled. (I remember thinking that without that facial adornment she would have looked so much better. But she was in any case quite a handsome woman and I could well see that given the lights and distance presented in the theatre she could have seemed to an audience quite beautiful.)

She said, 'Principal assistant, which means that I was produced from nowhere and disappeared at the wave of his hand, dear.'

Holmes asked, 'You were involved with the lion illusion?'

Her manner hardened, 'No, love, it was Pauline who played the princess, and she's dead. Listen, I'll tell you anything I know that might help you find out whatever it is that you want to know, except where it has to do with his secrets. I signed a contract to that effect and he always paid me well and treated me fair, so I'm not going to peach on him now that he is dead and gone!' With that she folded her arms in a slightly defensive gesture.

Holmes smiled at her, not unkindly, 'My dear lady, I will not of course press you upon this point, although the mechanical details of the apparatus and its use in perform-ance might be valuable. But in any case I have no official position in this affair, so instead let me ask you a little concerning Sigmund Neuberger himself. In questioning others I have gained an impression of great eccentricity; would you care to comment upon this?'

Her defensive manner relaxed and she laughed. 'He had his funny little ways but he certainly wasn't potty; far from it.'

I managed to squeeze in a question myself. 'How about his fixation with his dog, what did you make of that?'

She lowered her voice as she leant forward, the low neckline of her dress proving somewhat revealing. With her face only inches from mine she said, 'It was a bit of the old codology, mate.'

I was about to ask her what codology was but Holmes anticipated my question by saying, 'Ah yes, he was a show-man, we take your point.'

She turned to him and said, 'The dog was a good bit of showmanship, that's right. Oh, he was fond of the creature but then who wouldn't 'ave been; she was a sweet little bitch. But all this business about his life being over when she died was just a — how can I say — continuation of the newspaper stories that he got from her hotel suites and her picture being on his cheques and that.'

It was Greyshot who butted in at this point, asking, 'But Miss Latour, how about his other peculiarities, such as having his male assistants salute him in the street? Why I actually witnessed this myself a couple of times.'

She laughed. 'Yes, but you didn't see him give 'em an Oxford arf hour later and saying "thanks boys, have a drink with me." '

Greyshot was puzzled, 'An Oxford?'

She grinned, 'Oxford scholar, dollar, five bob!'

As we moved along the row, Holmes chuckled as he said, 'My dear Greyshot, east London argot is something which as a solicitor you would do well to study.'

He was puzzled. 'I have heard of rhyming slang of course but why did she not say scholar rather than Oxford?'

Holmes replied, 'That would have made it too easy to follow. For instance, if I asked you to fetch my tit-for-tat you would at once guess that I referred to my headgear. If however I called it a titfer, we would be bordering on a special language from which strangers might be excluded. It's really a simpler version of backslang as practised by east London butchers. In this particular street slang the spelling of words is reversed. For instance silly woman becomes yllis namow. I must let you see my monograph on the secret languages of the back streets.'

The tall, swarthy man, whose name proved to be Chester Schultz, had the speech of a North American and I tried to play Holmes at his own game, playfully perhaps expecting to expose some of his dialectic skill to be based on luck and chance. I asked Schultz, 'You are from Chicago, are you not?'

He shook his head, and Holmes said, 'Really, Watson, that observation has no foundation whatsoever. The windy city produces a speech which splits the words into short sharp fragments, as example Chi-ca-go, whereas Mr Schultz has the extended words of the mid-west, probably Missouri.'

'Yawl is close but ah come from jaist accrost th' Arkansas border.'

We discovered that Schultz had been brought from

America with Neuberger, where he had acted as the illusionist's assistant on the vaudeville circuits. 'Ah wuz with him right from the start, before he was the Great Lafayette; when he just had his protean act. Then when he started to build a big show with the illusions and all, he made me his number one in charge of the other guys.'

When we questioned him regarding the lion's cage and its manner of use he was no more forthcoming than Miss Latour had been. In fact he said, 'I look upon my giving him my word to keep his secrets as a sort of sacred oath. But anything else I can tell you that might help you I'll be glad to.' He confirmed the opinion that we had already received that Neuberger eccentricity was of the theatrical kind.

Holmes said, 'There was evidently method in his madness, eh Watson?' As we moved along to question the one man among the group from whom we received useful, not to say valuable, information.

Edward McGrath of the *Edinburgh Informer* was small and hawk-like in appearance, his clothing untidy but of high quality, with dark rung eyes and unshaven chin suggesting a sleepless night. Holmes took this obvious deduction a stage further, saying, 'Mr McGrath, I see that you have not visited your office, nor strayed very far from this spot since the tragedy occurred. The fact that you have a folded issue of the journal with which you are concerned tucked into the pocket of your greatcoat dated for the very night of the fire tells me this. Even had you been into the street you could not have resisted obtaining a more recent issue. You have been in contention with Neuberger, which I deduce from the admission ticket lodged in the band on your hat. Usually your press documents would admit you to the performance. Doubtless you are a critic as well as a reporter, for what other than an adverse criticism might have made you unpopular with the Great Lafayette.'

McGrath chuckled. 'Everything you have said is true, sir. My only contact with my editor has been by telephone from the manager's office, and in the recent past when I worked for a different journal in another city I did indeed rub Neuberger up the wrong way by writing about his performance and by suggesting that he was able to cause his lion to roar on cue. He was so defensive that I felt I must have stumbled upon something which he would rather not have known. Also he knew that I dearly wanted to find out something of his methods. He was no ordinary illusionist you know, for usually such people come to such magical greatness through conjuring and sleight of hand. Neuberger had no such background, having been a quick-change artist and sharpshooter. Is it possible that he discovered some element as yet undreamed of by stage magicians?'

Holmes was intrigued but obviously he needed to progress with his investigations. He said, 'Let us return to the events of that tragic night, Mr McGrath.'

The newsman nodded and said, 'During the second half of the show, I left my seat and sneaked in at the stage door, little dreaming that I would have no chance of leaving by the same means; for as you know the stage door became as impossible to negotiate as most others within minutes of the start of the fire. There was a banner hanging in the nearest wing, it read, "The Great Lafayette would appreciate it if those performers not actually waiting to make an entrance would stay off the stage during his performance.

Positively no visitors allowed." I used that banner, ironically, to hide behind! I wanted to watch the Lion's Bride from this vantage point rather than from the stalls. But no sooner had it got under way than there was a blinding flash from the lion's cage, and the poor creature was enveloped in flames and smoke. Neuberger was just making his entrance in his robes and carrying his sword. He too was almost at once engulfed.

'I tell you, Mr Holmes, as a newspaper man I have seen many fires but never one that started so suddenly or blazed up so quickly.'

Holmes asked, 'From the lion's cage you say, and not from the hanging lantern as has been suggested?'

He said, 'Definitely from the cage. Within a few seconds I could scarcely see my hand in front of my face for the smoke. I crouched where I was until the heat made me move. I tried to get out the way that I had come but there were burning spars of wood barring my way. In desperation I turned to try and make my way through the pass door into the auditorium but here I come to the most strange and alarming part of my story. The flames suddenly flared, illuminating the fact that my way was barred by the lion!'

We gasped at this statement. I asked, 'It had escaped then?'

He replied, 'Evidently and, as far as I could make out, the poor unfortunate creature was actually on fire, or at least its mane was. It reared up on its hind legs and waved its front paws at me and I fancied that eerie flashes of light emanated from its claws. I was terrified, both of the fire and the escaped lion. But I think the creature was my salvation because I retreated the only way I could, towards the safety curtain. As I did so I dreaded that I would be roasted, until

I discovered that there was a gap, where the curtain had not completely descended, having jammed against some obstruction. I managed to crawl beneath it and into the orchestra pit. Once in the comparative safety of the stalls I saw the flames starting to lick their way through the gap through which I had escaped, only just in time.'

Greyshot was the first to speak as McGrath appeared to have finished his narration. He asked, whoever would answer him, 'Is it possible that the lion was trying to signal that the pass door was blocked?'

Holmes chuckled grimly. 'I think not, for however intelligent a specimen he might have been, such communication is beyond the scope of *Panthera leo.*'

Greyshot said, 'But it was clever enough to return to its cage!' Even I allowed myself a smug grim chuckle at this point.

Holmes said, 'Ah, now you have hit upon a real mystery. How did the lion manage to get back into that molten twisted wreckage of its cage? But I must not indulge in irony, for it is clear that the lion did not leave its cage but was burned to death within it.'

McGrath retorted, 'You doubt my statement then?'

Holmes shook his head, 'No, I believe that you are yourself convinced of what you tell us but maybe there was another lion, illuminated claws and all!'

McGrath said, 'What happened to it then?'

Holmes smiled in a rather more kindly fashion, 'I have no answer as yet to that question, my dear McGrath, but what you have told me might well be of extreme value.'

We repaired, Greyshot, Holmes and I, to the Royal Caledonian Hotel for luncheon, over which we discussed, naturally, the findings of the morning. As we pored over the notes that I had made and the copy of Neuberger's will which Greyshot carried everywhere, the head waiter hovered. We enjoyed the Gullane Bay Cod with parsley sauce and Pommes de Caledonian, followed by an excellent raisin pudding and custard. We had washed it all down with some drinkable Alsace wine when the head waiter cleared his throat with an insinuating style and asked, 'Sir, d'ye ken the gentleman at the second table on your left, for he is also from London?'

Holmes smiled and replied, 'My dear fellow, in the largest city in the world, where literally millions rub shoulders I cannot be acquainted with everyone any more than you can know every inhabitant of Auld Reekie! No, I do not know the gentleman by sight.'

The waiter bowed apologetically and said, 'He is a Mr Will Goldston —'

But there my friend interrupted him, 'His name I could not be expected to know but I observe that he is on the staff of a large store and is possibly in a managerial position.'

The waiter started and said, 'Why, yes, ye are right but how did ye know that? He is the manager of a department at Gamages of Holborn!'

Holmes said, 'He is quite expensively dressed in clothing of considerable quality; yet their style is that of a decade ago despite their newness. His linen is particularly discreet for that of a man of his years, for he is no more than three and thirty despite his receding hair. His cufflinks, even his stock pin and watch chain have been chosen to blend with the background rather than to be displayed. He is dressed down as the professional shop worker needs to in order that his customers may feel superior. I noticed that when he entered he walked in the style of a shop keeper, just as you walk with the style of a waiter. When you bowed him to his table he said nothing but moved his head slightly to one side; the sure sign of a shop worker.'

The head waiter was still a little dubious, 'Yes, but how did ye know of his managerial position, Mr Holmes?'

Sherlock smiled and said, 'The fact that he is dining at the Royal Caledonian answers your question! Now Angus, may we have a large pot of your excellent coffee and would you please present my compliments to Mr Goldston and ask him if he would care to join us?'

Mr Will Goldston proved indeed to be of about thirty-two or thirty-three years old, prematurely bald with remaining wisps upon his brow which indicated that he had once worn his hair in a quiff. He crossed to our table and gave us that little gesture or mannerism which Holmes had pointed out to the waiter; the head slightly to one side in unspoken enquiry. He was lean, with well-defined cheek-bones and a hawk-like expression in his heavily-lidded eyes. He introduced himself, glancing shrewdly from one to the other of us with the air of a man who does not have too much time to spare. We all three shook hands with him and Holmes bade him sit down and accept a cup of coffee, which he did.

We sat and sipped the very hot aromatic liquid and Holmes took the plunge, saying, 'Mr Goldston, you are, I believe, the manager of a department in the world-famous Holborn store, Gamages?'

He replied, 'I am in full charge of that firm's conjuring

department; in other words I supply famous magicians with the impedimenta of illusion.'

He spoke in tones as precise as those of Holmes himself, indeed there were several points of similarity between the two men, save that Goldston spoke with what remained of a dialect. I could not place it but of course my friend could, asking, 'How long have you been away from your native Liverpool?'

Sharply he replied, 'About ten years, I was not aware that it was still there in my speech?'

Holmes said, 'Oh yes, it is still discernible, Mr Goldston.'

He was losing patience and said, 'Quite so, Mr Holmes, but what is the business? One does not invite a complete stranger to his table for coffee, having learned something of his background from the head waiter without having some kind of axe to grind.' Goldston took a watch from his waistcoat pocket and studied it.

I tried to lighten the atmosphere by saying, 'Be assured that we mean no disrespect, and have no wish to waste your time, Mr Goldston. My friends and I are greatly concerned over the tragedy at the Empire Theatre and imagined that you might be here in consequence of it too.'

Goldston paused before he replied, and Holmes said nothing but looked at me and I knew that which was passing through his mind, something to the effect that 'Watson handles these situations so well, it is one of the reasons why I like his company when investigating.'

At length Goldston relaxed a little and spoke. 'I came here to attend the funeral of Lafayette who was both a friend and a valued client. However, I was informed that this event had been postponed under extremely bizarre circumstances. I could hardly believe it when I was told that another body had been cremated in mistake for his own.'

Holmes asked, 'When did you last have contact with Neuberger, Mr Goldston?'

He replied, 'Personal contact? Oh, some weeks ago when he was in London. But I received a letter from him some forty-eight hours ago, perhaps the last he ever wrote. It concerned his requirement of several yards of teddy bear cloth of a kind which I had supplied to him before.'

Holmes interrupted, 'What do you think he needed this for?'

Goldston said, 'I don't *think*, Mr Holmes, I *know*. In his show he employed a tiny lady to impersonate a teddy bear. A second small person was being trained as a deputy, so obviously the material was to be used to fashion a duplicate costume.'

Holmes asked, 'Was the quantity ordered consistent with this requirement?'

Goldston became a touch devious, 'Well I mean to say, he may have wanted to make some spares as well.' Even I could spot the sudden return of a Merseyside tone to his voice. A raw nerve had been touched.

Sherlock Holmes spoke to Will Goldston with a re-assuring tone, almost as if calming a fretful horse. 'Come, sir, you can confide in me; I am merely trying to help Mr Greyshot here to recover for Neuberger's estate that which it is entitled to. I am not acting for the police and indeed I have no official capacity or responsibility being actually retired from active work. I have interrupted a fishing holiday to be here.'

But Goldston was still reticent, 'It is not a case of my

wishing to conceal information. My hesitance was prompted by professional ethics. I deal with a great many professionals who trust in my complete confidentiality when they order me to supply some item for a consideration. My artisans are likewise trustworthy, though to make doubly sure I give a piece of everything to a different workman to make, usually even in a different district and giving them only that section of the plans which concerns them.'

Sherlock Holmes whistled softly. 'I had no idea that the magic of the theatre required such secrecy but I applaud your professionalism. But you see if I were to ask you to reveal to me the mechanics and scenario of an item from the Lafayette performance I would not be doing so on behalf of some rival wonder worker, nor yet from curiosity. The police are hardly likely to be involved, but of course were they to be they would have less regard for your professional ethics than I have myself.'

The pause which followed was one provided by Goldston taking a packet of cigarettes from his pocket. He handled the cardboard packet with an ease that suggested that he did not normally use a case. He offered the packet to us each in turn. Holmes alone shook his head and the man from Gamages lit our cigarettes with a match. Then he enquired, 'Which particular item is it that interests you?'

Holmes, eager to catch Goldston's relaxed mood said, 'Why the lion's cage, sir, something of its mechanics would I feel be of enormous value, especially to Mr Greyshot who like myself has no connection with the profession you deal with.'

Goldston responded, 'Very well, I will give you the information you require upon the promise that you have already made.'

I do not intend to tire the reader with the details that Mr Will Goldston gave us, save those that are essential to the understanding of this narrative. Indeed I dare not, for at this time of writing Goldston is still in business. No longer manager for the Gamages conjuring department but as head of his own business Will Goldston Ltd with premises in Green Street, just off Leicester Square. He spent an hour altogether explaining the mechanics of the cage (his words augmented with many a sketch made upon the back of a menu) and also the way of the performance which was of course of paramount importance. 'The audience see the lion in a small cage at centre stage, pacing and roaring in a manner proving the animal to be the real thing. Lafayette enters in his oriental costume and carrying a sword. He is thrust into the cage and is at once attacked by the lion. He falls to the floor of the cage but to the amazement of everyone in the audience the lion rears up on its hind legs and removes a false headpiece, revealing itself to be in fact the Great Lafayette.

'That is the effect but in fact what happens is this. The real lion is taken mechanically by a combination of spring hinges and an optical principle into a hidden compartment in the cage. This same mechanism brings Lafayette into view, wearing a lion costume. Clever lighting makes the exchange unseen by the audience, especially as their attention is diverted by the entrance of Lafayette, or rather his double, at the right psychological moment. The double enters the cage and the rest is obvious with the real Lafayette removing the lion head.'

Greyshot asked, 'You mean, sir, that the people do not notice the change from the animal to the man?'

Goldston said, 'No, you see they have had ample time to accustom themselves to the real lion and then of course there is the diversion.'

We peered at the drawings and took in what we had been told but Holmes questioned one aspect of what Goldston had narrated. 'The double must have been more than convincing, and yet I have been told already that no person of actual striking likeness to Lafayette was involved.'

Goldston replied, 'Up to a minute earlier the real Lafayette had been standing before them in an exactly similar costume. The scenario presented to the audience was that he crossed to the wings to fetch his sword. The double, holding the sword at once replaced him and stood with his back to the auditorium. In the fastest change ever Lafayette donned the lion suit and secretly entered the compartment of the cage which would so quickly bring him into view. It was slickly done and always fooled the audience.'

Holmes nodded, 'And the authorities into cremating the wrong body! Tell me, my dear Goldston, how could the real lion be depended upon to move and snarl? After all, you have yourself suggested that this was necessary to prove its reality. Was it possible to train the creature to thus behave at every performance?'

Goldston looked a little shamefaced as he said, 'Why no, Neuberger took no chances. He had an electrical device installed under the steel floor of the cage which would give a series of mild electric shocks to keep Leo lively.'

As we shook hands with Goldston, Holmes thanked him.

'Mr Goldston, you have given us information which I feel sure will be invaluable in this unfortunate investigation.'

As the magical expert departed we retired to the coffee room where we sat, despite having already taken our fill of coffee. Greyshot said, 'I'm sure you meant what you said to Goldston, Holmes, but I fail to see how what he had to tell us had to do with the diamonds. I have to be quite sure that they are irretrievable before I can tackle the insurance company. Other than now having an inkling as to how Neuberger effected one of his mysteries I fail to see how any progress has been made.'

Holmes said, 'Exactly. You fail to see that which is right before your eyes. We have solved the riddle of how the lion managed to be in two places at once, for it was clearly Neuberger who stopped McGrath trying to escape through a blocked door. The real lion, poor brute, never left its cage in which it was roasted.'

I said, 'I suppose in all that smoke and excitement McGrath could have made that mistake.'

Holmes applauded, 'Watson, you excel yourself!'

Greyshot asked, 'Why then has the body of Neuberger in the burnt animal skin not materialized?'

Holmes said, 'That puzzles me still but perhaps it will yet be discovered. You have both missed another very bizarre aspect of McGrath's story, that of the eerie glow from the supposed animal's claws.'

I suggested, 'Some visual effect caused by the reflection of the flames upon the false claws?'

Holmes chuckled. 'The glow of fire certainly played its part but I'll wager the reflection was the light playing upon diamond rings!'

He had Greyshot's very fullest attention now, who asked, 'You mean the rings must have been still on his hands at that point; would they glow through the lion gloves?'

Holmes snapped, 'Through what the fire had left of them certainly. If they are still there they will serve to identify the body if we find it, and satisfy your firm at the same time, Greyshot.'

The solicitor was animated now. 'Do you think the rings will have survived the blaze?'

Holmes replied, 'Certainly the stones should. But I am also interested in finding the body so that the funeral can take place. Goldston has solved my other question, as to how the fire started; I'll wager an examination of the lion's cage will confirm my thoughts on that.'

Greyshot seemed a little ashamed that we should have thought him mindless of these things and said, 'Of course, the funeral and the cause of the fire, I did not mean to sound quite so single minded.'

Our return to the theatre was by way of a gentle stroll which took so much longer than it should have on account of Holmes's snail's pace of locomotion. I knew my friend well enough to know that his slow pace was not designed to annoy us; rather to give him the chance to mentally digest that which he had learned from Goldston. But, being who he was, he was able to keep up a quite irritating banter whilst exercising his grey matter. 'See the ravens, Watson? You won't see those in London except within the walls of the Tower, and would not even see them there save for the legend that our Empire depends upon their habitation. Rather like the apes of Gibraltar. Ah, there is a member of the clan Anderson in his full tartan and regalia. Did you know that the Scottish clan system was invented by a tailor who owned many bales of varying tartan material?'

It went on, like a recitation which we endured because we knew that there was method in his every word and deed. He reminded me at that moment of Shakespeare schoolboy who '. . . with shining morning face crept like a snail unwillingly to school'. Certainly Greyshot and I were anxious to gain our destination.

# CHAPTER FOUR

The inspector, even if not overjoyed to see us again, through a combination of pressure from Moss and some degree of common-sense was polite enough. 'Well, Mr Detective, how are you progressing with whatever aspect of this grisly business concerns you? For myself I think I may soon be able to officially cite the cause of the fire and the reasons for its effect, especially upon so much human life. I believe we have found all the bodies that we are likely to recognize as such.'

Holmes asked, 'Including that of Neuberger?'

The policeman shrugged, 'His remains must be there, among those remains that cannot be recognized. But Holmes, you may have other theories, and I use that word advisedly. For instance, how do you believe the fire to have started?'

There was no hint of mockery in my friend's manner but I knew him well enough to know it was there in his mind. He said, 'Doubtless just as you do, Inspector.'

The inspector chuckled. 'Ah, so we are agreed at last that it all began with the lantern?'

Holmes said, quietly, 'If that is your final thought, we differ still. I opine that the fire almost certainly started in the floor of the trick lion's cage.'

McCloud grunted with irritation and gestured to us to

follow him. He led us onto what remained of the Empire Theatre stage and pointed to the twisted mass of the cage. Then the Scottish sleuth smiled ironically and said, 'Show me, Holmes. I'm all agog to learn something from the great detective!'

Sherlock Holmes showed surprising strength and agility for one of his years as he picked up a lever and prised aside the twisted bars to gain access to the steel floor. Then he prised this up in its turn to reveal a series of electrical wires, their blackened extremities brazened to the steel through the heat.' You see, my dear McCloud, there was a short circuit which started it all.'

McCloud gaped at the blackened wires and plugs, 'What the dickens is this arrangement for? It does nay illuminate anything under yon steel plate.'

Holmes said, 'Its purpose was to keep the lion lively but instead it roasted him and his master to death. See where the flames must have licked through to the wooden portions at each end. It was smouldering unnoticed for a while before the fire erupted.'

The inspector was annoyed, 'Where do you get your information, Holmes? You had no more idea than I of this contraption being under the metal floor.'

Holmes chuckled, 'The head waiter at the Royal Caledonian was helpful in introducing an expert on such things.'

McCloud was furious now. 'Did yon expert tell ye anything else?'

My friend had mischief in his voice when he said, 'Yes, he told me to look for the body of a man dressed as a lion.'

Holmes and Greyshot moved on but as I lingered to take a last look at the short circuit which had started the tragic blaze I could not help but overhear McCloud say to his sergeant, 'Let him play, he's looking for a charred lion wi' a man inside!' There was some sarcastic sniggering.

At the back of the theatre we had to walk carefully through the fallen, charred battens from above and pieces of masonry and the very occasional piece of theatrical property that still glistened despite what had happened. Fire has that strange effect of destroying one thing and leaving almost intact that which is near it. We turned over collapsed lighting tripods and charred scenic flats in an effort to find that which an exhaustive search by the police had failed to uncover. We fanned out and again examined the stairway to the dressing rooms which had swiftly been made unusable by the fire. We also examined the only safety door that had been usable but which, at the time, had been inaccessible.

We returned then inevitably to the barred pass door to the auditorium which we at least knew as the last place that any witness could place Neuberger. (Even though McGrath had thought him to be a lion.)

Holmes studied the floor area in front of the door with renewed interest and evidently found something that he was seeking. 'You see, Watson, some faint trace of foot-prints beneath a covering of ash. Hand me your notebook, my dear fellow, and I will see what I can uncover.'

He examined near the ground where he fancied that he could see the very faint trace of footprints. Rather to my surprise we did soon perceive some rough prints as if made by a man wearing carpet slippers. Holmes smiled. 'See Greyshot, Watson, they look as if a man in slippers had allowed his toenails to grow out through holes in the toes.

Without doubt the footwear of the lion costume complete with claws.'

He was animated now, moving first in one direction and then in another, eventually following a faint pathway of prints. We followed and, on hands and knees, regardless of the damage to his clothing he tracked the path made by the dying man in the bizarre animal costume.

He led us first to the OP wing of the stage, and from there to the back wall of that side of the theatre. Then, near a charred piece of scenery he lost the trail but found it again when he raised it and cast it aside. 'You see, Watson, he was here before the fire caused that flat to fall.' His voice had the catch of great excitement, for he had found something which he considered very significant. The moved flat had revealed a square void in the floorboards — roughly square that is for the edges were charred and not regular. A dark space greeted our eyes as we gazed down through the gap. The floor around us seemed a little unsteady so we moved hastily back lest more of the floor should give way.

How such a gap should exist beneath the floorboards in such a newly finished building it was hard for us to fathom. Holmes called for a ladder to be spread across the floor and also demanded that one of the policemen should bring him a lantern. When this was shone down through the aperture there appeared to be a square flagstone, perhaps eight or nine feet below. This seemed to be the base of a sort of tunnel of earth and aged bricks.

One of the stagehands told us that he had worked upon the building of the theatre. He explained that the foundations had been based upon a seemingly secure square of flagstones, in turn based upon even earlier foundations.

Holmes said, 'Evidently not as secure as supposed. Neuberger must have used the flat as a shield against the flames but had the misfortune to stand over one of the flagstones which fell as a result of the heat. Now, gentlemen, I intend to descend through the aperture and see what I can discover.'

Of course, as an old soldier, I volunteered to make the drop myself but Holmes would have none of it. He allowed himself to be lowered by way of a loop of rope, taking the policeman's lamp with him. He was lean and lithe and swiftly slipped through the aperture whilst two burly policemen held the ends of the rope.

As soon as he called that he had reached the fallen flagstone we crowded to the edge and peered down. Holmes stood firmly and, evidently, quite safely. As he stood up straight, the top of his head was only about two feet below the surface, for he was more than six feet tall. He barely needed to raise his voice as he said, 'Please fetch the inspector, for he must be kept fully informed. Near my feet there is a gap about two feet high and almost as wide, framed by rough edges of ancient brickwork. What is beyond, through that gap I cannot and will not as yet say, for I feel that officialdom must be allowed to take over.'

When McCloud appeared on the scene he was, at first, mildly amused, thinking that Holmes had fallen through the floor during the course of his investigations but, when the full facts were given to him, he was serious and more helpful. Holmes told him of the second chamber which he was about to investigate and the inspector gave his blessing to this. Holmes and the light of his lamp again disappeared from our gaze as he doubled up and pushed his way through the jagged framed aperture. We saw and heard nothing for some minutes. Then Holmes reappeared without the lamp, which a ghostly glow through the aperture told us he had left down below.

He demanded that the inspector and Greyshot and I should follow him down, bringing with us extra illumination. We dropped down in turn, each reaching the flagstone and crouching down to get through the mysterious aperture in turn; first McCloud, then Greyshot and finally myself. We had to do it this way as the main aperture was so narrow. When it was my turn to make the drop, I was surprised that neither Holmes nor the others had called to me to give some intimation of what I might find when I joined them but I was, alas, to find out the reason only too soon.

I bent double again and followed the light into the second chamber. Once inside I found that there was sufficient height so that I could regain my upright stance. As I gazed at the sight that greeted me, my heart beat with unnatural pace and I felt a nausea that I have seldom encountered before. When you bear in mind that I am a medical man and have shared many a grisly sight during my association with Sherlock Holmes — quite aside from having served our late Queen in Afghanistan — you will appreciate the full meaning of that statement. What was the sight which met my eyes?

Well, dear reader, I do hope you are feeling strong enough to be given even my modified account of it. To begin with, I found myself in an apartment much larger than I had expected. It was in the form of a courtyard, perhaps some fifty feet long and twenty feet wide, lined with what appeared to be the frontages of places of business. Across their various façades were the faded slogans of an age long gone including an apothecary, a victualler and the like. There were glass panes with leaded lights but these were too grimy to see through. Upon the central area there lay more than a dozen bodies of men and women. I say bodies but they were more like skeletons really but with parchment-like skin over their bones and the rotted remnants of clothing partly covering them. There were children too, and they were all wearing the remains of raiment fashionable three centuries previous. Holmes alone stood seemingly in full control of his emotions, with Greyshot and the inspector holding their kerchiefs to their faces.

I took all this in slowly and with horrified disbelief. But there was another grisly surprise in the shape of a charred sacking bundle over which I had all but tripped.

Holmes broke the sepulchral silence. 'Watson, it is Neuberger, recognizable only by the diamond rings upon his fingers.'

I nodded, and asked, 'The others . . . are they actors from some restoration comedy, also trapped by some previous tragedy?'

Holmes said grimly, 'Not actors, Watson. These people were bricked into this tiny square by the authorities at the time of the great plague in order to save the larger number of Edinburgh's population from that scourge.'

A plague street. I had heard of them and even seemed to have read that there had been a number of them in Edinburgh but I had not expected that we would find one below the Empire Theatre. Carefully we examined the small alcoves which had been shops, where we found more bodies, some of them women and children, even a small baby. Of course, Holmes must have been as horrified as any of us at these gruesome discoveries but it did not seem to prevent his viewing it all in a rather dispassionate manner.

He explained to McCloud, 'These poor wretches would have existed for weeks before dying of starvation and thirst. You will perceive the remains of various foodstuffs in the alcoves, and a barrel which would have contained water. Another smaller one which was a wine cask they would have tapped only when driven by the madness.'

When I asked him to clarify this he asked, 'What is the first thing you desire upon awakening following an evening of wine bibbing?'

I cast my mind back to my army days and said, 'Water.' In saying this I had answered my own question, so I asked another. 'What will happen to all this when you make your find public?'

Holmes said, 'You had better ask the inspector, it is in his hands.'

McCloud said, 'These bodies will have to receive Christian burial but as for Neuberger, he is evidence as yet, though I am convinced that it is indeed he from the rings upon his fingers.' Holmes and I exchanged glances but did not comment upon the sheer neck of the fellow.

I hastily brought us to another aspect. 'Why do you think that, having fallen where he did, he made his way into this ghastly place?'

Holmes replied, 'Above him there were flames. He was close to dying from his injuries and instinct made him follow the light. If you shade the constable's lamp you will take my point.' With the lamp shaded we did indeed see a glimmer through a tiny aperture in one of the walls. He continued, 'I saw it first when I crawled through the gap. It is probably the wall that was built to imprison these poor creatures, for you will notice that the brickwork, although very old, is less ancient than the rest of the masonry.'

The doorman at the Caledonian did not recognize Sherlock Holmes, so disgusting had his raiment become. He saluted Greyshot and I smartly but put out an arm to bar Holmes from entering the lobby. He said, 'Carry on, gentlemen, ye can leave me to deal with the drunk. They are a problem here about but I'm used to it.'

Holmes pulled himself up to his full height and said, 'I rather think the alcoholic boot is on your own foot!' He squared up to the doorman with mock fisticuffs as he continued, 'Engine Eightpenny is just about the strongest ale short of being a spirit.'

The doorman at last recognized him and saluted. 'Excuse me, Mr Holmes, I didn'a know you in disguise. How did you know that I drink Engine Eightpenny?'

Holmes laughed, 'It has an aroma like no other beverage, my dear Forsythe.' (How like Holmes to know the doorman's surname.)

When Holmes joined us for dinner he was well scrubbed, with spotless linen and his jacket and breeches were free of seventeenth-century dust. He ate a hearty meal of fowl with a strawberry flan dessert whilst Greyshot and I sat and played with our food, daring to nibble just the least-rich morsels. I knew that Greyshot could see those parchment-covered bones of a bygone age rather than the roast duck which was placed before him; I knew this, because I could see them myself. The strawberries from the flan I could manage but mostly I just dreaded the thought of our discussion of the subject which I knew was still to come. I took my coffee black and strong, steeling myself for what was to be said.

Holmes broke the ice, sparing us any gruesome descriptive narration. He said, 'Gentlemen, I will not dwell upon the details of recent events, save to say that one can read of historic excesses without being in the least prepared for the sight of a genuine example. We are fortunate in that we need not concern ourselves actively with that which we have been forced to see, yet I for one will never be able to forget the sight of that plague street. Man's inhumanity to man is of course so often prompted by fear and ignorance, is it not?'

Eventually we did manage to bring ourselves to discuss the horror that we had been forced to see, and yet Greyshot seemed anxious to change the subject. Indeed he seemed rather on edge, which at the time I put down to that which he had been witness. However, he confessed to us that despite having recovered Neuberger's rings which had been so important to him he had another problem, perhaps of a rather more pressing nature.

He said, 'Gentlemen, I have another favour to ask which concerns Neuberger's will. I am of course fully aware of its contents and who will benefit and these are details which professional ethics prevent me from revealing, but I can tell you that I am in one whale of a hole and may end up in court for some kind of misconduct. You see at the time of the tragedy I was actually discussing changes and clauses with Neuberger which we did not have the chance to complete. Oh, the money with which to pay the beneficiaries is there — of that I am certain.'

He tailed off and Holmes said, 'I am glad to hear it for your sake, my dear Greyshot, but come man, put your cards on the table; you are among friends, are you not?'

Greyshot said, 'Well, you see Neuberger travelled the world a great deal and got the idea, rightly or wrongly, that his funds would be safer if deposited in safe boxes in various unconnected banks in a number of different countries. Now at our next meeting he was going to give me the names of these places and banks, in the strictest of confidence, but of course the tragedy has prevented this. Despite an exhaustive search the keys cannot be found, nor yet any written indication as to where they might be.'

I admit that what Greyshot had said was a great shock to me but Holmes took it very calmly. He said, 'My dear Greyshot, you do surprise me. You are trying to tell me that as Neuberger's solicitor you have no way of knowing where your client's money is banked? Oh dear.' It was his turn to tail off.

Greyshot blushed and said, 'Had he lived a day longer I would have had all the details that he had promised to give me. Of course I knew about the keys but have no idea as to where they are. They might even have been consumed by the flames.'

I tried to cheer him up by saying, 'If they were in the fire they might yet be found when all the debris from the theatre is sifted.'

Holmes nodded but said, 'I think a more logical place of concealment might yet be found. Our late friend in both of his personae — illusionist and financier — had very secretive ways, did he not? Why do you not take a stroll, gentlemen, and leave me to cogitate upon this problem, for like the Great Lafayette I too have a devious mind. I must learn to think as he did.'

Greyshot and I took Holmes's advice and simply strolled for about an hour. At first we tried to clear our minds from the problem in hand and behave like ordinary visitors to the great Scottish city and seat of kings. But it was not long before we had to admit that we were still mindful of our concerns regarding the Neuberger thousands, or even millions, whatever they might prove to be. We found our feet were taking us slowly but surely away from Arthur's Seat and were leading very definitely in the direction of the Empire Theatre, or rather what the flames had left of it. As we gazed at Matcham's now scarred masterpiece we wondered what stone or charred piece of rubble had been left unturned. Then it was that my gaze rested, not for the first time, in admiration of the big Mercedes with the words Great Lafayette artistically emblazoned across each of its doors. I noticed for the first time that the beautiful mauve motor car had upon its bonnet a silver mascot or statuette in the form of the dog Beauty. We looked at each other, Greyshot and I; our expressions told each of us that the other had thought the same thought! Greyshot was the first to speak our minds. 'Doctor, do you think it possible —'

He tailed off as I rejoined, 'I think it might be even probable!'

When he recognized us, the police constable who was guarding the car raised no objection to our examining the splendid saloon. There was nothing obvious to find so we raised the seat cushions and carefully searched those areas where the driver might have stowed his maps and gloves. We knew of course that anything obvious would already have been removed by the police, but knowing the inspector I fancied that he might well have overlooked some trifle. After much searching we found nothing of interest and were just about to give up entirely when I had a sudden inspiration. I pointed dramatically to the mascot and Greyshot, taking my thought, nodded his head energetically.

It was not difficult to unscrew the mascot, and having removed it from its mount I hastily turned it over, in the hope that it was hollow. It was and, moreover, there was a piece of paper within it. I could scarcely conceal my excitement or keep my hands still as I held the upturned mascot to allow Greyshot to remove the paper.

He handed the paper to me and held it up, savouring and therefore postponing the moment of unfolding it. I said, 'Excellent quality paper as one would expect, my dear Greyshot.' I held it up to the light where, even without opening it out, I could read the watermark. 'It says French. What do you make of that?'

He said, 'That it was made in France?'

I chuckled and said, 'I think not. It appears to be a trade mark, probably of a paper mill bearing that name. Ah yes, "Made in England" appears below the name.' I felt superior, and began to imagine how Holmes would feel when talking to me. I continued, 'It has been cut from a larger sheet, probably with nail scissors as you notice that the cut is somewhat serrated.'

Greyshot was losing patience with my Sherlockian impersonation, asking, 'Might it not be a good idea to open it and see what, if anything, is written upon it?

Abandoning my deductions, I spread the paper upon the car bonnet. The writing was extremely familiar to me:

My dear Watson,

I guessed that this might be the first place that you would look! The car has revealed no secret to me, save that the owner was extremely fond of chocolate creams and the chauffeur rather new to his job.

Greyshot and you must take dinner with me.

Your sincere friend,

Sherlock Holmes.

Greyshot looked rather superior as he said, 'It was astute of Mr Holmes to predict our actions. I understand about the chocolate crumbs but how did he know about the chauffeur?'

I was in no mood to explain so I just said, 'We have methods that are, perhaps, a little too technical for you to understand, my dear fellow.'

We resumed our stroll and spoke no more about the problems in hand. After all, Edinburgh has much to offer the visitor. But we thought that it might be better if we made no remark to Holmes concerning our investigations. My friend was no longer in the lounge of the hotel so I assumed that having beaten us to it with the investigation of the Mercedes he had either moved on to pastures new or returned to his bedroom to create a tobacco fog. Either way it was simply best to await his return.

# CHAPTER FIVE

That evening Sherlock Holmes surprised us both by inviting us to dinner at an Edinburgh restaurant as a change from taking it at the Royal Caledonian. At Hamish's they may not have exactly piped in a haggis but they gave us local Scottish delicacies, including the locally caught cod with stuffed potatoes and parsley sauce. We washed it down with some excellent hock and were tackling a Dundee pudding before the subject of the theatre of death was brought up again. I wondered if Holmes had made any other investigations following his patently obvious examination of the Mercedes, a matter which he had not as yet mentioned. At last he spoke. 'So you found nothing in the car, Watson?'

I suspected a bluff, asking, 'What makes you think that I have been anywhere near the car?'

He smile indulgently. 'Oh come, the washing and scrubbing has not removed all traces of engine oil. You read my note, of course, otherwise you would have no reason to keep silent upon your examination of the vehicle.'

I side-stepped by asking, 'What else occupied your afternoon?'

He said, 'About half an ounce of Scottish mixture. Do you know, for the first time since I left Baker Street I actually sat upon a pile of cushions on the floor whilst I inhaled the smoke. Such behaviour hardly seems apt at Fowlhaven but, for a serious answer to your question, I did make a few more enquiries around the hotel, especially among the retainers. They are a little more stoical than their southern counterparts but are fine honest people and extremely alert.'

The next day, shortly after breakfast, Holmes surprised me and, I feel sure, Greyshot as well when he suggested a visit to the mortuary for animals where the dog was at rest in her glass-topped casket. Our reception, at the pet's last resting place prior to interment, was polite though not ecstatic. The gentleman in charge said that he did not object to an inspection always provided that he was present. He said 'Only one other person has requested a last sight of our dear little friend. He brought a dog with him which, apart from the late Mr Neuberger, he assured me was Beauty's closest friend.' Holmes displayed no great surprise at this confidence.

As we peered down through the glass lid of the eerie little sarcophagus I was struck by the bizarre situation. The sad body of the lurcher was curled around the urn, presumably containing her master's ashes. The jewelled collar gave the poor little creature a strangely festive look, as if it had been decorated for Christmas, but Holmes read more into the sight than I did. He said, 'I notice, Watson, that the collar is encrusted with emeralds and rubies, yet those that I have questioned mentioned diamonds.'

I asked, 'Do you infer that the original collar has been stolen and replaced by a substitute?' He shrugged, so I went on, 'Surely a thief who did not wish his theft to be noticed would have replaced it with a copy, bearing fake diamonds?'

Holmes said, 'Perhaps not, if the theft were opportunist in nature.'

Greyshot argued saying, 'Oh come, Mr Holmes, surely your thief would not be carrying another gem-encrusted collar by sheer chance?'

Holmes glared at him, 'The collar may have been upon the neck of another dog and an exchange made. I believe there were other canines involved in the performance of the Great Lafayette. Notice, gentlemen, that the collar presently adorning the demised cur has been adjusted. It fits quite well but there is a scar upon the leather strap, showing that for some years it has been adjusted to be worn upon a larger dog. Greyshot, do the other animals wear collars adorned with precious or semi-precious stones?'

The lawyer replied, 'There are several of them and all had ornate collars, though not of great value like that worn by Beauty but, if we wait a little while, you will have a chance to speak with Chester Schultz upon the matter. He has orders to bring Duke, one of the other dogs, who will be chief mourner at Beauty's funeral.'

As we knew Mr Schultz was in charge of all dogs involved, it seemed worth waiting to see him. As we waited, I got a strange feeling that this whole episode was unwinding in a manner completely unsurprising to my friend Sherlock Holmes.

As the time for the dog's funeral drew nearer, there was much tutting by the undertaker and his staff as they opened the casket for the temporary removal of Lafayette's ashes. They explained that the ceremony, about to be carried out, was for the dog. 'Her master will be honoured in death tomorrow. Until then the ashes will not be returned to the casket.'

A few minutes before the appointed hour, Schultz arrived with Male, a very large dog, bearing a black material band around its neck, hiding the collar which must have been beneath. As the undertaker said a few words of praise for Beauty and her devotion to her master, Schultz gave Male a signal which caused him to sit up and place his forepaws upon the top of the casket.

I wondered at the time why Holmes had not confronted Schultz with his questions and suspicions before this ritual. Later the answer would present itself to me. As it was he quietly asked the tall dark American, 'Why have you switched the collars of the two dogs?'

Schultz started but recovered quickly. 'What makes you think that I have done that, sir?'

Holmes deftly removed the black material from the big dog's neck. He turned to Greyshot and me, saying, 'You will notice that the collar has been extended — with a new hole in the leather — to fit the larger neck of this dog.'

We could see that this was so and that a scar in the leather showed where the usual fastening had taken place. The collar was encrusted with diamonds and bore six silver bells, suspended around its circumference at intervals and between the diamond-studded areas. It would have been obvious, without the black crêpe cover, that a smaller collar had been adapted to fit the larger canine.

'Mr Schultz, kindly remove the collar so that I may examine it.'

It was an order rather than a request that Holmes made,

but the tall man shrugged and said, 'Remove it yourself, if you dare.'

It was Holmes's turn to shrug. He moved towards the dog but, as he did so, Schultz clearly gave the dog a signal. It snarled and reared up at Holmes, but Holmes had a way with dogs, as I knew from past experience and, as its paws rose toward his shoulders, he grasped its right forepaw in his left hand and kept a firm hold upon it. With his right hand he deftly unhooked the hole in the collar from its restraining projection and held the gaudily encrusted circlet of leather triumphantly aloft. The dog, bewildered, struggled to back away and Holmes allowed him to do so by releasing his paw. 'A little trick I learned from policemen who handle bloodhounds, Watson. The animal is unable to bite whilst its paw is held. It has some thing to do with reflex action.'

Ever correct, Greyshot asked, 'Should we not change the collars about?'

Holmes said, 'Not before we have carefully examined this one. Come. There will be ample time tomorrow to adorn Beauty again with her correct neckwear before the final replacement of the ashes.'

On our way back to the hotel, I dared to ask if some kind of complaint should not be made against Schultz, but Holmes shook his head. 'He can hardly be charged with changing about the two dog collars. I thought his device with the black crêpe was rather good, for even if it was seen through, as it was, he could not really be seriously accused of wanting to steal the diamonds.'

We repaired to Holmes's hotel bedroom to examine the collar more thoroughly. He laid it upon the bedside table and pointed to the sparkling decorations. 'You see, Schultz had not the shrewdness, facilities or perhaps the time to do what he should have done if he wished to keep the diamonds. These are the real thing; he should have had them replaced with jargoons. I am no expert, but even I can see that these stones are worth a quarter of a million at least.'

Greyshot searched his papers and then corrected him. 'Three-quarters of a million.'

I interjected, 'The silver bells must be worth quite a lot too.'

Holmes chuckled, 'I doubt if Schultz even considered their worth but, my dear Greyshot, they are worth even more than the diamonds.'

I was as perplexed by this pronouncement as was the solicitor. We both gazed in wonderment as Holmes shook the collar, causing the bells to give a tinkling noise. He asked, 'What causes the bells to ring?'

I said, 'A tiny piece of metal, shaped like a droplet, in each bell.'

Holmes smiled smugly (I thought). He said, 'Not shaped like a droplet, rather more like a key!' He turned the open end of one of the bells so that we might see within. Indeed, there suspended by a silver thread was a tiny key.

Greyshot reacted as if he had received an electric shock. He gasped, 'Do you think it could be that you have discovered one of the missing safety deposit box keys?'

Holmes chuckled. 'All six of them, I believe, my dear Greyshot.' He took his penknife from his pocket and, with one of its many devices, he prised open the closures at the top of each bell so that eventually he had a row of little bells standing on the table. Greyshot was all for instantly removing the keys from their bells but Holmes insisted that they should for the moment be left as they were. 'We do not want to confuse ourselves later as to which key belongs to which bell.'

I was puzzled. 'Is there then any significance?'

Holmes nodded, 'Quite probably, my dear Watson, for there is something about the bells which you have not remarked upon even if you have noticed it. If you look carefully you will see that each bell has a letter engraved upon it. Take my lens, if you need it, to assure yourself that it is so.' I looked through the lens at each little bell in turn and discovered that the letters were B, E, A, U, T and Y.

I said, 'Why, they simply spell the name of the dog.'

My friend grunted and said, 'That may be so but one never knows, Watson.' Greyshot's delight at Holmes's brilliant discovery of the keys was tempered by his curiosity to discover some indication as to the location of the locks which they might open. Holmes carefully removed each key and with some thin twine he tied each to the ring at the outside top of its bell. Then, having contented himself that each key was with its correct bell, he examined the keys in turn.

After a few minutes he said to Greyshot, 'There's nothing to be seen even with my lens to show where the appropriate locks are to be found.'

Greyshot said, 'When he mentioned the keys he not only failed to tell me where they might be found but also anything concerning the banks or other institutions where the boxes were located. He had inferred that he might be giving me some such information in the very near future.'

Holmes shook his head sadly, 'Alas, 'twas not to be. Keeping one's own counsel may be commended, yet has its disadvantages, as we now know.'

Holmes suggested that Greyshot should give him an idea of the itinerary of the Great Lafayette company over the two years that had passed, remarking, 'We are dealing with a very widely travelled and more than slightly eccentric individual; the smallest thing could give the answers we seek.'

Greyshot very quickly produced the travel particulars that Holmes had requested and then excused himself saying, 'Forgive me, gentlemen, but I have details to attend to concerning Neuberger's funeral. Also with that sad event being on the morrow I will be turning in at an early hour.'

We, however, Holmes and I, felt no such need for early slumber and 11 p.m. found us on the open-top deck of an omnibus, with my friend revelling in the fresh breeze and evening chill which was typically Scottish, even in springtime. His pipe produced clouds of smoke which must have given the bus the appearance of a locomotive from the street.

He spread the papers that Greyshot had given him and searched for that which he evidently wanted but had not expected to see. He stabbed at a list of theatre dates with his elegant forefinger. 'You see, Watson, there is a run of six theatres played one after the other in 1910 commencing with the Grand Theatre at Bolton, which is a prosperous industrial town in Lancashire.' I could not follow his point of interest, so he said, 'Look man, look at the list of towns which follow it — or rather the first five of them.'

I read aloud, 'The Great Hall, Exeter; the Empire,

Ardwicke; the Riviera, Ulverston; the Palace, Taunton; the Grand, Yeovil. By Jove, the first letter of each town spells out the name of the dog Beauty.'

Holmes nodded smugly. 'Exactly, and in each of those towns we will find a box which the appropriate key will fit.'

I was a little sceptical, despite the almost impossible coincidence otherwise presented. I said, 'But surely a theatre tour is planned for convenience of travel from one place to the next and for other reasons which would make this particular tour completely impractical?'

He said, 'For anyone less wealthy or eccentric than Neuberger you would be correct.'

The day of the funeral of the Great Lafayette dawned clear and bright, promising to be a perfect mid-May Sunday. The procession, despite the sadness of the occasion and the Scottish sabbath, evoked a Sanger's Circus parade rather than a funeral cavalcade. There were half-a-dozen splendid carriages, each pulled by a pair of handsome horses, from the heads of which blew plumes as if they were performing equines. The marching band played music which was neither grave nor gay and one felt that, at any moment, an elephant or an Eastern-decorated camel might appear. The glass carriage, with the floral tributes, bore wreaths from the great theatrical personalities of the day. Of course I knew who Little Titch, Marie Lloyd and Chirgwin were, but there were names less well known to me attached to some of the tributes. Greyshot told me that Rameses, Chung Ling Soo and Horace Goldin were well-known illusionists but I did not need him to tell me who Houdini was, for such was the American showman's fame that one could hardly pick up a newspaper that did not have his name printed there in some context or other. On this occasion the name was simply written upon a card, attached to a large wreath which had been made in the floral shape of a dog. The card read, 'To my friend the Great Lafayette, from the friend who gave him Beauty, his best friend.'

The sight of the tall, swarthy man at the graveside with the dog, Male, on a leash attached to a simple leather collar, made me have a touch of guilt and prompted me to say, 'Holmes, do you not think that Neuberger intended the diamond collar to be interred with the dog?'

It was, however, Greyshot who answered my question. 'Whatever he intended, and we shall never know his full intention now, those diamonds will remain in my safe until the estate has been settled. If those bank safe keys yield nothing, we may need to use whatever assets there are.'

No one had evidently noted the fact that the dog was wearing the wrong collar. It had, in fact, taken Sherlock Holmes to spot it and I doubt if another living soul would have thought about the matter. Nothing could be proven, I imagined, against our swarthy friend and the matter would rest, as did the bejewelled necklet, now safely in Greyshot's hands.

As Sunday is generally a day of rest, a goodly number of vaudeville people were present. Greyshot pointed them out to us. 'There is Sir Oswald Stoll who used to be in partnership with Sir Edward Moss; you see, they are together at the graveside, their differences put aside. The stout little fellow with the gold pince-nez is Horace Goldin, the famous Polish illusionist, and . . .'

Holmes interrupted him. 'But the man who sent the

most impressive floral tribute is not here. Is Houdini out of the country?'

He replied, 'Why no, I believe he decided not to attend the funeral lest his fame and celebrity should lessen the gravity of the occasion. After all, it is Neuberger's day. I have no doubt, though, that he will arrive later to inspect the tributes and be sure that his own is well positioned.'

Holmes asked, almost sharply, 'You do not like Houdini?'

Greyshot looked almost shifty, 'I have no reason to dislike him but there is something about him that has always worried me.'

The traffic in the particular part of Edinburgh involved was brought almost to a standstill as a result of the slow-moving carriages and the masses of people who lined the streets to watch. The funeral made newspapers all over the world with headlines such as, 'Lafayette and Beauty live together in death as in life'. Later, at the Royal Caledonian, the great and famous gathered to drink a farewell to their colleague and many were the stories exchanged regarding the strange showman and his many eccentricities.

Later we revisited Piershall and saw some of those who had not attended the private funeral inspecting the tributes. Prominent among them was a short, thick-set man wearing a fine Saville Row suit which was so creased that he could have been sleeping in it.

Greyshot introduced Harry Houdini — the renowned American jail breaker — to us. 'These gentlemen are Sherlock Holmes and his colleague Dr Watson.'

Houdini smiled archly and said, 'Sherlock Holmes needs no introduction or build-up, which I assume is why you didn't give him one?' It was, I suppose, intended to be some sort of joke but its point rather eluded me. But actually the introductions were not necessary anyway as some ten years earlier we had both met Houdini, and through the years would have more dealings with him though, at the time I speak of, this was to be far into the future.

Holmes asked the American, 'What did you make of Neuberger, as a man and, of course, as a showman?'

Houdini smiled, a little harshly I thought, with what one might term a professional smile and replied, 'As a showman, he was possibly second only to myself, with the exception of Billy Robinson who calls himself Chung Ling Soo. Where I give them danger and a hint of death he gave them colour, spectacle and lots of Sousa marches. As a man, well that was different; he and I got on well.'

Holmes brought up the subject of Beauty. Houdini responded in a way which rather surprised me. 'The dog? Well, we were both playing at different theatres in some town about ten years ago. Bess, my wife, had picked up this stray dog and wanted to keep her but I didn't agree. So we bathed the animal, brushed her until she looked presentable and gave her to Sigmund as a gift. At first he treated her just like a dog but, in time, obviously he got this idea of putting her on a pedestal thinking it would appeal to his fans — and it sure did.'

I'll be honest and say that at that time I could see little value for Holmes in this discussion with Houdini but afterwards he said to us, 'So, Watson, Greyshot, it was as I suspected. The dog was purely for show and publicity. Neuberger was not as eccentric as was supposed. I had suspected this but it was good to have it clarified.'

# CHAPTER SIX

Sir Edward Moss flicked the ash from his cigar carefully into the ashtray on the coffee table in the hotel lounge. A self-made man; a showman but one who acquired manners and decorum as well as wealth on his way up the theatrical and social ladders. He spoke with authority tempered with a hint of curiosity. 'Mr Holmes, I understand from young Greyshot that you have been of great service to him in his effort to make something out of the affairs of our late friend Neuberger. Greyshot reckons that you are something of a miracle worker. Well, I am much in need of a few miracles myself. You see I have not only lost one of my very best drawing cards in the death of the Great Lafayette but I have also lost my beautiful new theatre, which was to have been the jewel in the Moss Empire crown!'

I asked, 'It was insured though, was it not?'

But it was Holmes who said, 'Really, Watson, that is a fatuous remark if I may say so. Sir Edward can be compensated for the loss of bricks and mortar but nothing can quite make up for the inconvenience and loss of income which has been brought about by the fire.' Then, turning to the great impresario, he said, 'Sir Edward, you mention miracles; yet I have worked one for you already.'

Moss started and enquired, 'Pray, what is that, sir?'

My friend chuckled, saying, 'Why the discovery of a plague street beneath your property. Are you not astounded and intrigued by that which it has disclosed?'

Moss grunted. 'It is, I am sure, very interesting to historians and archaeologists and the like but not much use to a beleaguered showman.'

Holmes stabbed the air with a long, thin, accusing finger saying, 'You are wrong there, sir, for once they are appraised of its discovery, the public will be lining the block around the theatre in order to get a glimpse of the gruesome scene that lies beneath floor level. The public are always attracted by the macabre, I would have expected you to realize that.'

Moss worked hard on his cigar before he replied, then eventually he said, 'I take your point, sir, one which as you say a showman should have appreciated. All those mummified bodies make a grisly sight and could be made the more dramatic with the right lighting. Why, as you say, I could have them lining up to pay a shilling a head to see it all. Especially when I tell them that speed is of the essence and that it is a once-in-a-lifetime experience. After all, as soon as the builders are brought in, the gruesome place will need to be sealed up again. By Jove, you are a showman at heart, Mr Holmes. The business lost a great potential impresario when you decided to become a sleuth.'

Holmes chuckled and said, 'Well, Watson has always assured his readers that I would have made a great actor, purely on the evidence of a few disguises that I have been forced to adopt at various times, but I have never been told that I was a showman.'

The theatre magnate intimated that he was indebted to

Sherlock Holmes for his brilliant business suggestion but, far from brushing aside these expressions of gratitude, Holmes said, 'I do have a favour to ask you, Sir Edward. Here is a list of theatres played by the Great Lafayette in recent weeks. You do observe something strange about it, do you not?'

Sir Edward screwed his monocle into his eye and peered at the paper which Holmes handed to him. Then he said, 'Why yes, this itinerary is known to me of course and is as big a mystery to me too. These theatres are not geographically placed to form a practical six-week run; oh, he managed it, I know, but he turned down a sequence of my London theatres and provincial theatres which would have been a far more sensible tour. I just put it down to the fact that the man was an eccentric. After all, you have heard of far more bizarre examples of his actions already.'

At this point I wondered if Holmes would take Sir Edward into his confidence concerning the six bells and their keys but he did not, instead amazing the impresario with a demonstration of his uncanny powers of deduction.

He said, 'Above all else, Sir Edward, do not let these events of the last days affect your health. Take your doctor's advice concerning the imbalance of your glands. He may have mentioned this when he prescribed for your liver spots. Please, when you take the holiday which he also suggested, do be sure to visit a temperate zone rather than that place in Turkey where you are apt to dally whilst on holiday.'

The impresario dropped the monocle from his eye as these last words were spoken. He gasped gently and then said, 'Upon my word, I was first tempted to think that you knew my doctor. But I know him well enough to know that he would obey his Hippocratic oath at all times. Your colleague is a doctor. Has he noticed something about me and mentioned it to you earlier?'

Holmes replied, 'Not at all. I'll wager he is as surprised as you with my pronouncements concerning your health. The imbalance of your glands is indicated from your eyebrows, or rather the appearance of them. They barely stretch to a position above the outer corners of your eyes; a sure sign of gland problems. That you consulted him regarding liver spots is indicated by your use of a cream which covers, though does not remove, them. To take a vacation in a hot climate is just common sense for a man suffering from skin blemishes and your past visits to Turkey are indicated by the preponderance of Turkish silver in your personal adornments; your watch and a ring and, I'll wager, your cuff links too. The watch chain was, of course, obtained separately in Europe.'

I had not noticed the telltale darkness of the silver items but little ever escapes Holmes's gimlet eyes. Sir Edward Moss was astounded by the demonstration of Sherlock Holmes's medical knowledge, all of fairly recent discoveries. When I said as much, Holmes said, 'I cast an eye now and then over your medical journals, Watson. You brought a few with you on our fishing trip, if you remember?'

During the week or so which followed, Sherlock Holmes and I travelled a great deal in our quest for the missing boxes. Bolton, in Lancashire, was our first port of call — so to speak — and there we consulted all the principal banks, showing them our first key, without any sort of success. At all these financial institutions they expressed great surprise at the extreme smallness of the key.

The manager of Dalton's bank for example said, 'I feel that the safety deposit box involved was made especially for a client, perhaps by a private finance company.' Of course, he could give us no clue as to where we were to find such an enterprise. 'We disapprove of such firms, Mr Holmes.'

As we strolled down the main street I asked, 'Where does one start with such a quest?'

Holmes said, 'From wherever Neuberger started, Watson, which is the Grand Theatre.' We soon found the theatre which, whilst not as ornate as some, was none the less a neat and prosperous enough looking venue for music hall and vaudeville. Enquiries told us that we would be able to see the manager, a Mr Phelps, just before the first house, in the lobby. 'Aye, you'll know it's 'im by 'is toppat an' cigar!'

At six of the clock we duly presented ourselves in the theatre lobby, which by now was filling with good honest North Country folk, intent upon being beguiled by singers, comedians, jugglers and Captain Anchor's Wonder Sea Lions. The manager, Phelps, was indeed unmistakable as he stood, top-hatted, cigar-smoking, nodding and smiling with joviality to his regular patrons. He was stout, red faced and looked a trifle smug. 'Appen I can 'elp thee, lads?'

Holmes smiled ingratiatingly and handed the manager his card. The joviality dropped a trifle, 'Oh I see, pros are ye? Sherlock Holmes. Now that sounds familiar. What do you do, cross-talk act are you? Well, if you want to go in on your Wilkie you'll have to wait until I see what seats are unsold. You know the score, boys, you must have been in the business a long time judging by your ages.'

Holmes managed to put right the false impression that we had created — that of two resting professionals wishing to see the show free of charge through showing a card. As we followed him to his small office, I enquired of Holmes, *sotto voce*, 'What did he mean by Wilkie?'

Holmes replied, equally softly, 'It is theatrical argot for card. Wilkie Bard is a popular comedian, and bard rhymes with card.'

Phelps, impressed by Holmes's real identity, when it was revealed, and the impressive vocation that he followed, seated us in the little room with its framed professional portraits and faded showbills proclaiming in some cases long-forgotten popular favourites. He seated us comfortably enough and poured three shots of Johnny Walker into a trio of suspect glasses. 'Who were you interested in, Lafayette? Oh yes, he was here just a few weeks ago . . . dreadful tragedy. Poor old Sigmund!'

He spoke the first name of Neuberger with obvious attempt at effect and to impress us. He continued, 'Of course, we've 'ad 'em all here, you know . . . George Robey, Marie Lloyd, Wilkie Bard, Little Titch. Oh yes, they've all trod these boards.' He climaxed his monologue with a sweeping gesture which took in the photographic portraits, all signed by their subjects to Mr Phelps — The best manager on the circuit — and even more familiarly to Dear old Frank. He deposited his cigar on an ashtray, took a drink from his glass and said, 'Through your teeth and round your gums, look out stomach, 'ere it comes!' Then he took a red silk bandanna from his pocket and belched, hardly managing to conceal that fact with the silken square.

He blew his nose with trumpet-like alacrity and then

said, 'I don't know why it is that I'm so popular with my artistes. I think it's just my refinement. That's what a theatre manager needs — refinement. Now lads, what is it you wanted to know?'

Holmes asked, 'You were pretty friendly with Neuberger, obviously, so it occurs to me that he might have imparted to you some confidences.'

Phelps seemed flattered. 'Oh yes, well he did impart a few confidences.' Then he became a little guarded. 'It's not a matrimonial matter is it, I mean *cherchez la femme* and all that?'

When reassured that it was not matrimonial, he relaxed again and said, 'He was very secretive, used to have visitors in his dressing room and would not say who they were, and for certain they were not there to have him sign photographs and such. There was a fellow who called several times, and' (he assumed an air of some pride) 'he was somewhat conspiratorial. Would have done well as a spy in a melodrama. Little short, dark fellow wi' a foreign accent and cloak.'

We managed to get Mr Frank Phelps to allow us to examine the dressing room which had been occupied by Lafayette only a few weeks earlier. It was currently being used by the star of the present show, the distinguished ventriloquist, Arthur Prince.

As he knocked at the door of dressing room number one, Phelps told us, 'Mr Prince is a real gentleman, tha' knows. Always first one of the artistes to enter the theatre each night, even though he's late on the bill, being star turn an' all.'

We were invited to enter, which we did and were introduced to a tall, well-built man of handsome appearance and gruffly polite manner. He was attired as a high-ranking naval officer and had keen eyes and seemingly a very fine head of dark brown hair.

He studied Holmes's visiting card and his eyes twinkled as he said, 'Allow me to introduce my wife. Daphne! Come out as soon as you can, there are some people I would like you to meet.'

A voice answered, 'Coming, dear . . . just fixing my hair!'

Prince held converse with his wife, evidently behind a screen in the corner of the room. She had a pleasant contralto and I waited for her to step out from her place of concealment but, to my surprise, Holmes said, 'A remarkable exhibition of ventriloquism,' Mr Prince. You throw your voice to perfection and there is no perceptible movement of your lips.'

Prince said sharply, 'How, then, did you spot my little prank?'

Holmes replied, 'I detected some movements in the muscles of your throat and neck but, sir, it was well done, an exhibition to which a little more distance would have lent enchantment.' But I still couldn't believe that I had been fooled by a ventriloquist, so I drew aside the screen to reveal what at first appeared to be a young lad in a sailor's uniform. A second glance showed that we were looking at a puppet of the kind used by vocal illusionists.

'Meet Jim. He's been all over the world with me, haven't you, Jim?' Prince stood beside the figure.

Then the dummy spoke in a most lifelike fashion, saying, 'Cor blimey, guv'nor, not arf I ain't. Who's the thin-faced bloke with the long nose?'

Prince reprimanded Jim. 'You must not insult Mr Holmes, he is a famous detective.'

Prince replaced the screen and said, 'Well, Mr Holmes, I've given you a demonstration of my art, perhaps you can give me one of yours. I'm told that you can tell quite a lot about someone through the science of deduction?'

What Holmes then said might strike the reader as being a trifle impolite but I suppose Jim had sharpened his manner somewhat by personal remarks.

Holmes said, 'Well, Mr Prince, despite your dress I note that you have not served in the Royal Navy, and that you started to lose your hair at a very early age.'

Prince started, 'Everyone else assumes that I have been a genuine naval officer in my time, and as the other gentlemen will confirm I have an excellent head of hair.'

Holmes said, 'No ex-naval man would wear a soft collar with his uniform, and your excellent head of hair is in fact a transformation, one of the best I have ever seen, all but undetectable save for the faint scent of spirit gum (and I note that your stage make-up does not include any false whiskers) and the presence of the wig block upon your dressing bench. Mr Phelps mentioned to me your unusually early arrival at the theatre before each performance. So you see I was already half expecting to find some kind of preparation of a secret nature. I'll wager you always arrive here wearing a hat.'

Prince was no longer sharp of manner and his eyes twinkled in admiration of the detective's art of deduction. 'How did you know that I started to lose my hair when quite young?'

Holmes said, 'Baldness is a slowly developing process, you are still less than middle aged, yet the transformation is quite a full one.'

'Well, upon my word!' The ventriloquist was both amused and amazed by Holmes's demonstration, and made to place the detective's visiting card carefully between the wall and the mirror which was screwed to it, alongside other pasteboards that were wedged around betwixt wall and glass. Unfortunately the space between engulfed the card, so it fell behind the glass. Holmes watched this action and its consequence, almost at once taking his penknife from his pocket and with one of its attachments attacking the screws.

I was as surprised at this action as were the ventriloquist and the theatre manager. I said, 'Holmes, do you not have another card to give to Mr Prince?'

Phelps said, 'He can have the one you gave me if you haven't another for Mr Prince.' Sherlock Holmes still disregarded all of our assurances regarding the lack of importance in the matter. Eventually he was able to lift the mirror down from the wall and there was a corresponding flutter to the floor of not only the card which Holmes had given to Prince but of several others.

Sherlock Holmes scrambled upon the carpeted floor with an agility surprising in a man of his years and, among these several pasteboard squares evidently found what he was looking for. There was a gleam of triumph in his eyes which perhaps I alone among us could detect. He said, 'It may be just a trifling thing, gentlemen, but it may help me with my enquiries. Mr Phelps, Mr Prince, pray forgive me for removing the mirror from the wall. Do not worry, I will soon replace it.'

As I held the mirror in place Holmes quickly replaced the screws, inserting a vesta in each hole to make a snugger fit. When he had finished he said, 'There, it is safer now, certainly in the matter of elusive visiting cards!'

That night we put up at an inn, where in the lounge bar Holmes showed me his prize. 'You see, Watson, I am confident that Neuberger lost this card behind the mirror a few weeks ago, just as Prince lost mine.' He showed me the card:

**Locks and Safes Constructed**
Silas Silvano
28 Khyber Passage
Bolton, Lancashire

'What do you make of it, Watson? You know my methods, please apply them.'

I examined the rectangle of card carefully, then said, 'Well, it is cheaply printed upon inexpensive card stock, which allied to the lack of prosperity which rings from the address given, would point to a not very successful trader.' I handed the card back to him and he squinted at it again through his lens.

He enquired, 'Nothing else?'

I shook my head and he smiled, a trifle smugly I thought. Then he said, 'As always, you look, Watson, yet you do not see. There are other more interesting points, raised by this card. He who proffered it was clearly a purveyor of the trade of locksmith and probably of modest dress and appearance; however, I detect a certain sense of guilt regarding his appearance. You will notice that he has used the corners of the card to clean behind his finger nails. You see the deposit, whilst minute, is partly composed of tiny iron filings. In other words you will expect to find a man with the hands of an artisan but with a conscience regarding the appearance of his hands, possibly manifesting itself at the last possible moment. He is of mixed parentage and not afraid to admit it.'

I asked, 'How can you tell?'

He replied, 'Silvano is an Italian name, probably his father was Italian and his English mother got her way by christening him Silas!'

Holmes never failed to amaze me, and yet irritate me at the same time with such examples of his uncanny powers of observation. Though full of admiration I was as ever frustrated at my own lack of observance. Of course the visit to Khyber Passage was still in the future, yet I just knew that it would prove him correct in these details regarding Mr Silvano.

The following morning found us at Khyber Passage in search of Silvano who proved to be a small, earnest-looking man inhabiting, for business purposes, a small lock-up workshop full of the implements of a metal worker. He was dark and with the bright eyes of an Italian. As he spoke to us, he moved his hands in a furtive manner as if trying to clean one finger nail with another. 'What's up gents, lost your keys?' It was obvious what the bread and butter of his trade was.

Holmes said, 'No, I am more concerned about strong boxes, of the kind which would be opened with one of these.' He showed Silvano the keys.

Silvano's eyes grew round and very large. 'Might I know who you are, sir, and by what right you are in possession of keys which I recently made for another gentleman who demanded absolute confidentiality?'

I chipped in, 'The gentleman for whom you made these keys is no longer in the land of the living. Did you not hear about the death of Lafayette?'

Holmes clicked his tongue at me in irritation and asked, 'What name did the gentleman concerned give you? Come, you can speak freely for my name is Sherlock Holmes and this is my friend and colleague, Dr John H. Watson.'

Silvano seemed somewhat taken aback with disbelief followed by an expression of plain old-fashioned surprise. He said, as he put down a file, 'I suppose you can prove to me who you are, gentlemen, because anyone tall and beaky could walk in here and say what you have said. I'll grant you look like who you say you are but it pays to be careful in a confidential line of work.'

'Quite right,' Holmes agreed as he took letters addressed to himself from his pocket and a faded photograph of himself upon the steps of 221B Baker Street. But Silvano was still doubtful.

Then Holmes said, 'How long is it since you lost your bull terrier, Mr Silvano?'

The locksmith jumped. 'How did you know about Buller? If you must know he died about six weeks ago. Sixteen he was.'

Holmes nodded. 'And you could not bring yourself to get another dog despite the rats.'

Silvano scratched his head. 'How did you know his breed?'

Holmes said, 'His collar and chain still linger on the floor in the corner. The word Buller is engraved in quite large letters upon it. It is a name usually associated with bull terriers.'

Silvano nodded. 'And the rats?'

Holmes said, 'Look!' Then he stamped heavily upon the floor and a grey-brown streak which darted from beneath one bench to the other told its own story. 'You must get over your grief for the loss of your dog and get another one before the rodents become too numerous for comfort. I detected the rats' droppings upon the floor when we entered.'

The bright-faced little fellow smiled an open smile and said, 'Guv, I'm convinced, so how can I help you?'

Holmes said, 'Well, if you can give me any kind of information regarding where the strong box concerned is lodged, I would be greatly obliged.'

Silvano looked thoughtful and said, 'Well, sir, I am of course a man to be trusted, otherwise my clients might fear that I had made duplicate keys. But they don't actually tell me as a rule exactly where the boxes are placed. If I was to hazard a guess I would tell you to try at the New Cincinnati Bank in Alma Road. It is the kind of place where a gentleman of a secretive nature like Mr Sherman . . . yes, that was the name he gave, would use.'

Holmes asked, 'Was he of small stature with gold-rimmed pince-nez?'

He nodded in agreement, 'That's him, Mr Sherman.'

The manager of the New Cincinnati Bank, of obvious American origin, was less co-operative than Silvano. He said, 'You realize that anyone might come here with some penny ante story like yours, gentlemen? I mean I had never heard of the Great Lafayette; the guy came here with the name Sigmund Neuberger and wanted us to store this strong box that he himself had had constructed. Now already I have divulged to you far more than I am supposed to.'

Holmes started to produce his credentials but the manager, a Mr Putnam Van Duck, waved a hand and said, 'I don't doubt that you are who you say you are, that's not the point. If you were the Archbishop of Canterbury or the Prime Minister the matter would still be confidential.'

We had for that moment to leave it there. But Holmes wired his brother Mycroft at the Diogenes Club and a second visit to the New Cincinnati Bank proved more fruitful. Holmes remarked, 'Watson, I believe I told you before that Mycroft not only works *for* the British Government but on occasion *is* the British Government!'

The manager produced the box with a rather surly style. 'OK, so you've got friends in high places but there was no need to rub it in!'

He left us to examine the box in seclusion and it opened easily with the key from the B bell of Beauty's collar. The box proved to contain about five thousand pounds in currency, and nothing else. We returned to Edinburgh where we handed the box and its contents over to Greyshot who, whilst delighted with the fruits of our labours, was as concerned as I with what a slow and difficult business it would prove to recover all the boxes.

'Mr Holmes, you might not so easily discover where the others are lodged.'

Holmes, who had blanched at the word easily (with justification because it had not been a simple matter) said, 'I have no intention of undertaking such a series of investigations unaided. Now if you will forgive me, Mr Greyshot, I have work to do and wires to send.'

His manner was a little terse and Greyshot was apologetic in his tone. 'I am most grateful, and if my firm can reimburse you to a larger extent than envisaged, rely on me to arrange it.'

My friend glanced down his long thin nose at the solicitor, saying, 'I claim no fee at all, for I am retired, a pensioner entirely through my own frugality and enterprise.'

Over steaming cups of coffee in a workman's cafe (Sherlock Holmes had catholic tastes), my friend explained to me what he intended to do. 'Watson, in Exeter I have residing a trusted ex-irregular (you may remember Thompson) and in Ardwick — which is a suburb of Manchester — I have a grateful ex-policeman whose job I was able to save. In Ulverston there lives a trusted ally of mine from cases long ago and, as luck would have it, Lestrade is presently spending a long-overdue holiday in Taunton. This leaves only Yeovil, where a Madame Helene has a promising clientele.'

I gasped, 'Her occupation?'

He chuckled. 'She is a private investigator, possibly the only female of the species, with whom I have had some correspondence over the last five years. Do not look so disapproving, Watson. Our sex could not forever hold the profession to itself, any more than an individual such as myself could forever be entirely alone in the field.'

The days that followed were a nightmare of activity, or would have been for anyone other than Sherlock Holmes. Wires were delivered, read, answered and dispatched, it seemed, almost by the minute. For once in his career, Holmes did not himself follow up any of the leads but merely advised by wire. He was the interlocutor, controlling it all from the Royal Caledonian Hotel, Edinburgh.

The first of these New Irregulars to present himself to Holmes in person was Inspector George Lestrade, late of Scotland Yard. He proved to be much as I remembered save a little grizzling of his hair and whiskers. He was indeed as down to earth as ever. He took dinner with us and gave some account of his adventures.

'Well, Mr Holmes, it was easier for me than you might suppose, given my police training and the fact that I still have effective documents. Scotland Yard sometimes consult me on certain matters. I took your point about going to the theatre where this Neuberger had performed, under his stage name. I was told there that a tall, dark fellow had been round there calling himself Sherlock Holmes but that his identity had been questioned. However, he had gone so far as to ask to see Lafayette's dressing room. Now listen to this, Mr Holmes, I was evidently hot on his heels and had only missed him by hours and was told that he had got a large dog with him.

'The manager of the theatre had been foolish enough to point out to him a chair in which this Neuberger had sat during his week there but which had not been used since. This evidently through superstition on account of what had happened to him. Evidently the dog had sniffed at the chair and the dark chap had left soon after, with the dog seeming to lead him on some sort of hunt.

'Well, Mr Holmes, call it luck but it was the sight of the big dog rather than the chap himself that attracted my attention. I shadowed them from the town centre until the dog led the fellow to a sort of mews where various small tradesmen had premises. He eventually went into the premises of a Ruddendale Financial. I waited for him to emerge and then after a decent interval I went in and put my cards on the table, including my police credentials. The fellow in there seemed a little bit shifty but he showed me a box which was deposited there by a Mr Castang. I have brought the box, and I only hope it is the one you are looking for, as I don't really relish taking it back.'

Holmes opened the box easily with the relevant key. Again a substantial amount of money was disgorged plus, this time, some jewels and bonds. These were received gratefully by Greyshot.

I wish I could tell the reader that all six boxes yielded up their secrets as easily. It was true of those at Ardwick and Ulverston but Thompson in Exeter had a far-from-easy time in finding the box required. When he presented himself to us, I was astounded at the change in the appearance of the urchin of the London streets that I had known of yore; here was a quietly-spoken young man of thirty with the slightest trace of a London accent. He said, 'Cor, Mr Holmes, you've sent me on a merry dance you have. Do you know the theatre where Lafayette played only a week or two ago had already been demolished to make way for a picture show? I soon discovered the Hotel Splendid where he had stayed that week. The head waiter told me that he had noticed Neuberger (though he did not of course call him that) going off for a trip in his Mercedes one afternoon with a box-shaped parcel. More enquiries told me of the spot where he had descended from the car and dismissed the driver. I hung around there and eventually discovered that he had gone into a restaurant where they remembered him. An eccentric gent, they called him. One waiter said, "He came in the front entrance bold as brass and sneaked out after his meal through the kitchen. Carrying a square parcel he was, and he was a hefty tipper!" '

Thompson continued, 'There was mud about that had obviously been there for some time. I saw some tracks with those Cuban-shaped heels like the foreign boots. I followed the tracks and found myself near a seedy-looking building where an Acme Finance Company had an office. It said outside, Loans and Advances Arranged. I went in there and, to cut a long story short, they had the box you wanted and I knew it was his because of the description that the seedy bloke gave as soon as I mentioned your name. Then I wired Mr Mycroft who sent a local police inspector who gave me permission to bring you the box. Got a lot of go in him still, your brother, eh Mr Holmes?'

Thompson refused to take the money which Holmes offered him, saying, 'But for you gents, I'd have turned out a sneak thief or hooligan. As it is I'm in business on my own as a turf accountant.'

We had a conference with Greyshot and he, and his company, were of course delighted with the recovery of the boxes and their contents. He said, when we had given him most of the information at our disposal, 'Obviously it was Schultz whom your agent shadowed, going by the general description and the fact that he had this very large dog. Old Male always had a good nose, rather like a blood-hound.'

Holmes nodded. 'Yes, and although I never confided in him concerning the bells and keys he may already have had some inkling of the existence of the deed boxes. He was acquainted with that run of theatres and may be shrewder than we at first thought. Fortunately he has not been able to beat us to any of the boxes. Of course one box remains — that which we believe to be in Yeovil, Somerset.'

I asked, 'How is your lady detective progressing?'

He replied, 'Her wires and one detailed report have not been encouraging. This is not from want of effort upon her part but Schultz will be on his way to Yeovil if not already there, so Watson, the game is afoot!'

I had never visited Yeovil before, so I looked around me with interest as we journeyed in a seedy taxi cab from the railway station to the office of Madame Yvette Helene. The lady proved to be of smart, though not beautiful, appearance, her age perhaps three-and-thirty. She had only the faintest trace of her accent of her French origin.

She said, 'Mr Holmes, despite much investigation of the theatre where Neuberger appeared and the hotel where he resided, I have gained no sort of lead as to where he might have opened an account or lodged a strong box. However, I have seen — and even shadowed — your tall dark man with the large dog. I have learned from this only that he has somewhat bizarre interests.'

Holmes's eyes brightened. 'Bizarre? How bizarre?'

She said, 'Well, whilst following him, always in different guises I have noticed that he was always carrying, either in his hand or under his arm, one of a number of different books on the occult. Also on one occasion I came upon him on a park bench, experimenting with a needle dangling from a thread, as if dowsing for something.'

Holmes said, 'He may have some sort of lead based on information which he has gained. If we had that, I feel sure that we could benefit from it.' Sherlock Holmes worked hard upon a cigar, forsaking his pipe out of consideration for Madame Helene. At length he said, 'I have a rather preposterous idea. Schultz is greatly interested in the supernatural. Could we not set up some sort of clairvoyant's booth and lure him to it that we might try and gain the knowledge that he has upon the subject?'

Madame clapped her hands. 'Wonderful. There are some empty shops very near to the boarding house where he resides.' I could see that the whole idea captivated their imagination.

Madame Helene did not divulge to the agent — who represented the owner of the chosen shop — her true identity or purpose. Of course the agent was a little surprised that she should want the shop for only a few days but when she offered a handsome rent, her request was not refused. We put up at a hotel quite distant from these premises and Holmes and I kept well in the background. A signpainter soon produced an eye-catching placard:

**Gipsy Rose**
Fortune teller and
clairvoyant extraordinaire

We draped the window with black cloth with the placard in its centre, then arranged the inside of the shop in such a manner that Holmes and I could see and hear, without our presence being observed. Madame Helene made a good job of her disguise as Gipsy Rose, with scarves and ear rings. She sat behind a small table upon which were the tools of her trade: a crystal, some playing cards, a writing pad and pencil.

During the first day no one stepped over the door mat

for a consultation. On the second day a small, worried-looking woman entered, obviously with a problem. Madame Helene discovered what the poor woman's problem was with a few well-chosen enquiries. Then to my amazement she solved the matter with a few words of really sensible advice. The problem was of an intensely personal nature and I have no intention of divulging it to the reader. Enough to say that the poor woman left as if a ton weight had been taken from her shoulders. I was on the point of congratulating Madame upon her wisdom and kindliness (needless to say she had made no charge for the advice) when she hissed, 'Quick, get back behind the curtain!' Schultz entered the trap warily. Madame asked him for a fee of five shillings.

'Cross my palm with silver . . .' and it all had a ring of authenticity. He sat, peering earnestly at her as she gazed into the crystal. She said, 'You seek something which you know to be near but cannot find. You think I can help you to find it. Well, I am merely the earthly representative of psychic forces. These forces will need a lead of some kind, for the agencies of the occult have all time, space and eternity itself to control. Wait.' She raised a mittened hand. 'I see a square object and a small distinguished-looking man. He wants you to give me some sort of link or connection between you.'

He looked blank at first, then asked, 'What is he wearing?'

She said, 'An overcoat with a velvet collar. He has gold-rimmed pince-nez and a little dog.'

He gasped, 'It is him, it is . . .' He pulled himself up short of speaking a name. 'He did leave a message . . . but I cannot understand it.' He rummaged in his pocket and brought forth a scrap of paper upon which some letters had been written. He said, 'I cannot allow you to handle this or copy it. . . .' He was clearly uneasy.

Madame said, 'Have no fear, I do not even wish to know what is written upon the paper. Just hold it against the crystal and all will be clear to those in the other world.'

He did as she bade him, whilst she covered her face with her hands and muttered incantations. Then she said, 'Now hide it carefully, let no one see it but tell me the circumstances by which you got it.'

Schultz looked a little shifty. 'He . . . he wrote it on his dressing room bench, then said he wanted me to keep it safe in case anything happened to him. He died and now I want to find out what it means.'

Helene asked a great many more questions, the answers to which we listened to with great interest. Skilfully she managed to manipulate him so that he revealed several points that were of great interest to Sherlock Holmes.

Schultz asked her, 'Does the crystal tell you anything about a ruby ring, set on a platinum band?'

She said, 'I see a ring, worn by the man with the gold pince-nez during his earthly life.'

He faltered, 'Oh, then it was not hers . . . not Nadine's?'

She said, 'It might have been Nadine's: he wears it in another world perhaps as an omen. It may be not very far away.'

He said, 'Ah, then it is in the box after all.'

Eventually she told him that the crystal was clouding over. 'We can tell no more from it at present but if you start out for the place which first occurred to you at exactly twelve of the clock tomorrow, some force may guide you.'

After he had gone, grateful for the advice, Sherlock Holmes congratulated the lady upon her guile. 'My dear Madame Helene, that was a performance to rival anything by Sarah Bernhardt. You have placed him where he will give us an opportunity to shadow him tomorrow, and I assume you glimpsed that code when he placed it against the crystal?'

She said, 'Yes, I was greatly helped by its powers of magnification. I can write upon this pad exactly what I saw.' With deft strokes she wrote upon the table. It was a series of numbers:

40 16 10   50 10 30 44 18 24   4 30 48   18 38
46 18 40 16   6 2 36 40 10 36.

I was amazed that the lady had been able to remember these numbers from just a glance and said as much. But it was Holmes who answered, 'Watson, Madame Helene has something with which I would dearly love to be endowed — a photographic memory. I'll wager that she has already deciphered the message.'

The lady gave a bird-like bob of her not unattractive head. 'That is right. It is the simplest known code, with each letter of the alphabet given a number. A is 2, B is 4, and so on through to 52 for Z.'

I asked, 'As it is so simple, why could Schultz not decipher it and why, I wonder, did Neuberger write it down?'

Madame Helene said, 'They are perhaps both of them less gifted than we imagined. I could believe it of Schultz but Neuberger possibly felt that anyone who saw the paper would not know to what it referred but I also wonder why he bothered to write it down.'

Holmes chuckled, 'I once knew an American gentleman who opened bank accounts in almost every town he visited. He suffered a dread of poverty in later life. But that poverty came sooner than expected and he needed to trace the money. In many cases he had completely forgotten where it had been deposited. I was able to trace many of his accounts but some of them will remain forever a secret. Perhaps Neuberger feared a failing memory.'

The message that Madame Helene had written was clear enough: 'The Yeovil box is with Carter.'

I asked, 'I wonder who Carter is?'

Holmes rebuked me. 'You are assuming that Carter is a person's name.'

I replied with a question, 'Aren't you?'

He said, 'Not necessarily, Watson. Carter could be an occupation as there are many thousands of men who ply their trade as carters in Britain; even in this motor-ridden age there are possibly a couple of dozen in this area.'

The local police and postal authorities were unable to furnish us with the address of anyone named Carter who operated any kind of bank, financial business or poste restante service. After some hours of investigation along those lines we were forced to fall back upon Holmes's original impression that the trade of a carter might be involved. Our enquiries in that direction proved to be exhausting. Holmes had been right as there were far more of those who plied their trade with horse and cart than imaginable. We found those who took packages and sacks from the railway station, those who aided farmers with extra loads to carry and some who did not even ply for trade but were known by reputation.

I could, dear reader, write for your perusal a monograph titled, 'The Carters of Yeovil'. Between the three of us, for several days we discreetly investigated everyone who plied that trade within a twenty-mile radius. Schultz seemed to be having no more good fortune than we did.

Then came an evening when I was, for once, thrown upon my own resources. I left Holmes at the hotel, in a brown study, obviously not to be disturbed, whilst Madame was busy with another of her cases. I slipped into a tavern, near the railway station and, pausing only to purchase a copy of the *Evening Bugle*, ordered a tankard of the local brew which proved to be a rather strong cider. I turned the paper over to glance at the small advertisements upon the back page and from long force of habit found my gaze directed to the personal column. 'Will relatives of the late Colonel Graves contact Messrs Clive, Blunderstone and Clive . . .' etc. All were strictly run-of-the-mill announcements, save one which took the form of a limerick:

> He stood on the bridge at midnight,
> His lips were all aquiver.
> He gave a cough, his leg fell off,
> And floated down the river.
>
> Carter

My heart pounded as I began to feel that there was perhaps a connection with our quest, the clue being the addition of the name Carter to this, otherwise seemingly meaningless, doggerel. The bridge at midnight might, I thought, indicate some sort of tryst for that very night. I finished my cider and sped by cab back to the hotel, only to find that Holmes was missing from our rooms. He had left no sort of message for me nor yet any clue as to where he might have gone. I decided to take things into my own hands, asking the clerk at the reception desk where the nearest bridge might be.

He said, 'The nearest of any size is over the River Yeo, or rather one of its several branches. It is not far.' He gave me the directions I required.

I determined to be on that bridge at twelve of the clock. Meanwhile I made preparation for my excursion, making sure that I would have to hand a lamp, compass and my service revolver. Having decided to take a short nap, in case of a long night of activity, I was awakened by the chiming of my travelling clock. I stopped it deftly and leapt from the bed. The clock told me that it had been accurate in awakening me at eleven exactly.

Despite the mildness of the spring night, I decided to wear my Inverness cape as this garment provided me with ample pockets for my essential items of equipment. A brisk walk brought me to the slope up to the bridge. I prepared myself for a long wait, making myself as invisible as I could. There were no vehicles around and few persons crossed the bridge during the half hour which followed.

Then suddenly I saw Schultz, walking on the bridge travelling towards me from the side opposite. Although the street lamps made it barely possible to make out his dark complexion, it was bright enough for me to see that it was him. The very large and distinctive dog was made to sit

111

beside him as he paused at the centre of the bridge. He stood there in silhouette, his spare figure in the partial darkness making him look like some child's matchstick man. I hardly breathed as I observed him, hoping that he would not notice me at all.

The minutes ticked by until my hunter told me that it was five after midnight. Nothing seemed to disturb this single strange shadow. I supposed that Schultz had also seen the advertisement and had reached the same conclusion as I had. Yet were we both present and possibly as a result of some foolish ruse? My reverie was disturbed by the appearance of another player in the drama. A short, stout man, bewhiskered and wearing a billycock hat came upon the scene. He was carrying an oblong package, box-like and covered in brown paper. The two figures met at the centre of the bridge and the shorter man handed Schultz the package, tipped his billycock and retreated the way he had come. But he no longer interested me.

I was anxious to confront Schultz and relieve him of his wrapped box. I was willing to show him my revolver if he refused to part with it. As I strode towards him, Schultz began to retreat in the opposite direction to the far bank of the Yeo. I fairly leapt in pursuit but as he broke into a run I could scarce keep up, hampered by my game leg. I could soon see that I had lost all hope of catching up and apprehending him. I dropped back and crossed the bridge again determined to find Holmes and tell him of the turn of events.

I had missed a golden opportunity to apprehend Schultz in the act of receiving the strong box which must have been the property of the late Sigmund Neuberger. I wondered how I would tell Holmes without making myself seem foolish or incompetent. Perhaps I was both.

After such an incident, a second chance for redemption seldom occurs. Imagine, therefore, my astonishment when I espied Schultz and his dog at the end of the bridge which I was now nearing. I realized that he must have crossed the river again at some other point and expected me to continue in the direction in which I had been moving. But I had no time to puzzle the dilemma as to how he had managed to double back.

He saw me running toward him and, strangely I thought, he hesitated rather a long while before resuming his flight. As I chased him again I noticed to my annoyance that he was no longer clutching the wrapped box. I wondered as I ran if he had hidden it somewhere or perhaps handed it to some confederate.

Soon I was near enough to him to shout, 'Stop, stop there, Schultz!' with the expectation of his hearing my words, for his hesitation had lost him some space between us despite the length of his legs and the lameness of one of mine. However, lose him I did in the most likely yet annoying manner. He turned a corner so that he was out of my sight and when I, in my turn, rounded it he was nowhere to be seen. There were several turnings that he could have taken and I suppose by sheer ill luck I picked the wrong one.

Of course I retraced my steps and tried another turning but they all had that irritating winding feature which made it impossible to see just where he had gone.

In my dilemma I tried to apply the sciences of my friend Sherlock Holmes in tracking my quarry. I searched with the aid of my lamp for footprints of both man and dog and did by that means eventually find the turning he had taken. I followed his trail and then lost it at a main street which was neatly paved and of course unyielding to the prints of canine or man.

How can the reader fully appreciate my frustration? Well, perhaps he can if taking into account the surge of triumph that I had experienced upon witnessing the exchange of the package. I had swelled with pride to think that my discovery of the advertisement had led me to all but a brilliant conclusion to my detective work. I had fallen down, though, when it came to being the man of action that I needed to be at this eleventh hour.

Sherlock Holmes, with his long sinewy limbs could have caught Schultz red-handed but I comforted myself in the thought that Holmes had not been available for me to inform of the discovery that I had made. Surely I told myself, I had done the best that a lame, ex-army medical man in his late fifties could be expected to do.

As I dragged myself slowly back to the hotel I considered the events of the night and then quickened my steps in the thought that the sooner I could tell Holmes what had occurred the better. Although he would justifiably blame me for losing our quarry, he must surely applaud my deductions of the earlier part of the evening.

There was little chance of finding a cab at one in the morning, so I resigned myself to a long weary trudge. By the time I reached the sight of the hotel my leg was giving me severe pain but that discomfort instantly evaporated when I saw Schultz, complete with hound and package, actually entering the premises in which we were staying.

My mind reeled. Was he undergoing some change of heart and planning to surrender the box to Holmes?

As I entered the hotel, I was just in time to see Schultz's figure following the dog as it bounded up the stairs. Ignoring the sleepy night porter, I rushed in pursuit and caught up with Schultz just as he was entering Holmes's room. The dog was evidently already inside that apartment. The fellow was just about to close the door on me as I made an energetic entrance. Holmes was nowhere to be seen and I could only assume that Schultz had obtained the key for there had not been time for him to force an entrance.

I shouted, 'Where is Holmes, and what are you doing here, Schultz?'

He spoke gruffly, as if suffering from a throat malady. 'Doctor Watson, I thought I caught sight of you earlier but could not be sure.'

I snapped, 'You well know that I was in pursuit of you, sir. Now I have caught up with you no matter what your purpose here. You will kindly place that box upon the table and then raise your hands.'

As I spoke, I whipped out my service revolver and levelled it at him with a reasonably steady hand. However, the dog caught me unaware and bounded at me, forcing me to the ground and knocking the revolver from my grasp. As it spun across the floor Schultz retrieved it and I cursed the fact that I had quite forgotten the dog in my excitement. As it was it lay there with its two enormous paws upon my chest and its great slavering jaws but inches from my face. Its breath was none too sweet but that was perhaps the least of my troubles. Then to my surprise Schultz called the creature off me.

He said, 'Here Prince!' and I recollect wondering that he had called it by this new name as he bade me rise to my feet. Then to my utter amazement he offered me the revolver, holding it by the barrel and extending its handle that I might grasp it. I pulled myself together and brandished the returned weapon, saying, 'Oh, so you surrender then?'

What happened next was one of the surprises of my, not uneventful, life. He spoke but with Sherlock Holmes's voice, 'Come, my dear Watson, surely you have no plan to shoot me?'

I gasped. 'Holmes, can it really be you?' He chuckled as he answered my question with actions rather than words. He cast off the mackintosh — so like the one that Schultz was usually seen to wear — then the dark wig, and then taking a towel and some grease, began to remove the dark pigment from his face.

I was a little petulant as I enquired, 'It was you, then, who took the box from the mystery man on the bridge, Holmes? I understand the disguise, and I assume that you also solved the riddle of the personal advertisement but how did you get hold of Schultz's dog?'

He chuckled. 'My dear fellow, one Harlequin Great Dane is very like another, save that this one is called Prince rather than Male. I hired it from a breeder. It is an amiable creature despite its size and formidable strength.'

There were still aspects of the whole situation which puzzled me. 'How did you manage to double back across the river and appear, minus the box, causing me to chase you in a different direction then, and why indeed did you run from me to start with?'

He laughed. 'I will answer the second part of your question first; I was not running from you but I had a colleague with a dog-cart awaiting me on the far bank. When I saw your light and heard a shout I confess that I did not realize that it was your good self but imagined that it was some cohort of Schultz's. When you entered this room and brandished your revolver all became clear.'

I grunted then said, 'That does not explain your reappearance on the other bank. How did you cross?'

He smiled enigmatically, 'I did nothing of the kind. I returned here in the dog-cart, crossing the river at a spot at least a mile from that bridge.'

I was furious. 'Do you doubt the evidence that my eyes presented me with? Why, I even followed your tracks for a few hundred yards!'

He shook his head, 'Not mine, Watson, but I deduce that the real Schultz, with Male, appeared to keep the appointment that I had already kept. He was late, possibly having only just solved the riddle of the bridge at midnight.'

I gasped. 'So it was the real Schultz that I pursued? I wondered what he had done with the package.' Of course I should have realized that I was scarcely likely to have discovered some lead in this affair that had escaped the gimlet eyes of the world's greatest detective.

To say that we burned the midnight oil thereafter is slightly inaccurate for we burned that of two and three in the morning in discussing the events of that night. Then, when I went off to my bed at three-thirty I was accompanied by the huge Harlequin Great Dane.

Holmes told me that he himself needed a good night's sleep — or what remained of one. For a man who usually appeared to need the minimum of slumber he seemed suddenly very keen on dozing comfortably and I suspect that he just did not wish for the canine company!

Prince insisted upon sleeping on my bed and produced an untypical ferocity when I was unwise enough to attempt to remove him from it and, consequently, I was forced to sleep uneasily in an armchair.

In furnishing all these details I have perhaps been guilty of keeping from my reader those facts concerning the contents of the brown paper-wrapped strong box. This proved to contain several thousand pounds of currency of the usual British kind, plus a great many gold coins minted in an obscure African republic. These later proved to be of immense value and must surely have been smuggled out of their country of origin.

Breakfast was made slightly uncomfortable by the presence of the dog, which was well trained in some respects yet seemed to have table manners to match those of his slumbering habits. I was certainly relieved when he was returned to the dog breeder from whence he came!

We returned to Edinburgh where we surrendered the last of the boxes to the delighted Greyshot. He had news for us. The inquest had been held on the death of Sigmund Neuberger and other members of the Lafayette company. Verdicts of death through misadventure had been returned, with no hint of foul play and little mention of the escapade which had led to the wrong body being cremated. Of course this verdict made everything the smoother for the reading of Neuberger's will, and made possible without delay the insurance payment to the Moss Empire company. This would of course enable the theatre to be restored, if not even further improved.

We decided to take a last look at that Theatre of Death before we departed from Auld Reekie. The builders' wooden scaffolds were already being roped into place across the theatre façade. To one side, a gap had been left and a tunnel of sheet iron constructed to form a safe entrance. People were entering through this in considerable numbers and buying tickets at a hastily-constructed box office. Above this newly augmented way a sign read:

WHILST THIS THEATRE IS CLOSED FOR REBUILDING PATRONS ARE INVITED TO VISIT THE PLAGUE STREET WHICH HAS BEEN SEALED SINCE 1669 AND ONLY RECENTLY DISCOVERED BY THE EMINENT DETECTIVE SHERLOCK HOLMES. PRICE OF ADMISSION IS ONLY 6d FOR ADULTS AND 3d FOR CHILDREN AND SERVANTS. TICKET HOLDERS MAY MAKE THEIR WAY THROUGH A SAFE AND SECURE TUNNEL WHICH PASSES BELOW THE THEATRE OF DEATH WHERE THE GREAT LAFAYETTE AND SEVERAL MEMBERS OF HIS COMPANY RECENTLY DIED IN A HORRIFIC FIRE

As we passed through the tunnel and into the grisly apartment below the street, Holmes turned to me and said, 'I wonder what else is left from this tragedy to line the Moss Empire's pockets, Watson?' We were soon to learn what that might be. There was an egress through a freshly-drilled wall and another tunnel. Beside this aperture was another box office and a fresh example of the busy signwriters' work:

A FASCINATING RELIC OF THE GREAT LAFAYETTE. AN EXTRA CHARGE OF 2d FOR PERSONS OF ALL AGES AND CLASSES IS MADE FOR THOSE WHO WISH TO SEE ONE LAST ITEM OF OUTSTANDING INTEREST

We each dropped two copper coins onto the table and were ushered through a similar walkway to the one through which we had entered the plague street. We found ourselves emerging into a courtyard at the rear of the theatre itself. There stood Lafayette's mauve Mercedes, with a uniformed chauffeur standing smartly beside it. In the back lounged Sir Edward Moss, sporting a cigar and raising his hat to each new group of people as they arrived. Photographs of the great illusionist were being sold at a stall and a photographer was offering to make a likeness of anyone who wished to be photographed standing beside the Mercedes.

Holmes muttered, 'Ashes in the egg-timer, Watson, ashes in the egg-timer!' (I knew he alluded to the anecdote of the widow who had her late husband's ashes placed in an egg-timer, claiming that as he had never worked in his lifetime he might as well be forced to do so after his demise!) 'I feel sure that Neuberger will create as much wealth for Moss as he did when he was a live theatrical attraction.'

# EPILOGUE IN PERTHSHIRE

We were back at our trout stream in Perthshire or, at least I was, for my friend was sitting upon the bank smoking his pipe and in a sort of trance, whilst I fished. I was irritated that so many days of my holiday had been taken up with the Lafayette affair but knew that Holmes had enjoyed the interruption. A few days of contemplation on a river bank was enough for Sherlock Holmes.

Suddenly I espied a rowboat which seemed to be making straight for our particular spot on the bank. It turned out to be carrying friend Greyshot who brandished a brown envelope. We greeted him as warmly as we felt we could a man who had used such a lot of our spare time.

He handed the envelope to Holmes, saying, 'My company wish to reward your services, Mr Holmes. I remember what you said before concerning your scale of fees; indeed I believe you even allowed your long-time retirement to affect your judgement of this affair. You have retrieved for us an enormously large legacy of cash and valuables without which we could not have completed the requirements of Neuberger's will. Therefore, I implore you to accept this payment.'

Holmes took the envelope and studied it carefully. Then it handed it to me and asked, 'What do you make of this, Watson? After all, you know my methods.'

I looked carefully at the thick envelope and studied the hand-written words 'By Hand. Sherlock Holmes, Esq.'

I said, 'It is written by a man of most definite decisions. I deduce this from the forceful style with which it is penned. Other than that I see little of note.'

Holmes nodded, 'As usual you see nothing where much of note is to be read before even opening the envelope. It is, on the contrary, written by a man who is more than inclined to change his mind about much in life. He changed his mind twice over this very epistle. Notice the writing, started with a waverley pen and then finished with a relief nib. You took this change of pressure and style to be part of a determined hand, Watson.'

I said, 'Very well, so he changed his mind concerning which pen nib to use but what other change of mind did he make?'

Holmes turned the envelope and pointed to the gummed flap with the stem of his pipe. 'You will notice that the flap has been sealed then hastily re-opened and resealed. When he resealed it, a larger thickness was contained, causing that gum deposit to be visible.'

We both looked to Greyshot to act as adjudicator.

He smiled, 'You are absolutely right, Mr Holmes, in every detail. Our Mr Grace, who was given the unenviable job of arranging for your payment did indeed change his mind regarding the nib with which he fitted his penholder. (He is not a user of the quill as do some still employed in law firm offices.) He placed three hundred pounds in banknotes inside the envelope, sealed it, and then decided that your services better deserved five hundred!'

We invited Greyshot to stay and dine with us at the inn and he accepted the invitation. I showed him the large trout that I had hooked and he seemed a little bit timid concerning the dining upon it.

'You don't mean to say that we are going to eat this poor creature at the inn?'

I said, 'Either this or some just like it that another angler has hooked. We all hand our catches to the landlord each night, it is traditional. Mind you, anything of outstanding size or interest we keep to hand to the taxidermist.'

Holmes and Greyshot exchanged glances of disgust at the whole idea. Holmes commenting, 'I, too, prefer not to have met my dinner before I eat it, my dear Greyshot.'

Our host was delighted with my trout but, I thought, I detected an air of worry in his usually sunny face. He was a large and ruddy-faced man, doubtless made larger and ruddier by the day through the consumption of his own ale. But, worried or not, he provided us with a first-class dinner of trout, fried potatoes and parsley sauce. This was followed by an undoubtedly handsome suet pudding served with piping hot custard and slices of fruit.

As he cleared the empty plates and brought our after-dinner brandies, Holmes took the envelope from his pocket, saying to him, 'Landlord, I wonder if I could impose upon you to place this envelope into your overnight safe. It would put my mind at rest.'

The landlord flinched a little, and said in am embarrassed manner, 'I wish I could accommodate your request, Mr Holmes, but you see my safe has been burgled and forced open and I cannot use it at all now.'

The landlord led us through to his office which was behind the public bar. He gestured dismally toward the small safe with its open door and burst lock.

Holmes grunted, 'Upon my word, no finesse. A smart safe man could have opened a simple safe like that as easily as you or I could set a grandfather clock.'

I asked, 'Was a very large amount taken, sir?'

The landlord replied, 'That is the only fortunate thing about the affair, Dr Watson. The takings had been delivered to the bank only a few hours earlier so there was but a very few pounds involved; trade having been slow last evening.'

Sherlock Holmes was, I thought, a little guarded of manner as he said, 'Well, at least you do not need to go through the mental anguish of assuming that some member of your staff or — even worse — a member of your own family was involved.'

He brightened, 'Really? How so, Mr Holmes?'

My friend said, 'Well, all such persons would be aware of your banking arrangements, would they not? You are looking for a rather unskilled burglar, possibly one who simply followed an impulse.'

The landlord assumed a rubicund expression of entreaty as he began to ask, 'Mr Holmes, I suppose you wouldn't consider . . . ?'

But his words were cut short by a curt reply from a mildly irritated Sherlock Holmes. 'Your supposition, sir, is entirely correct!'

As we sped London-bound on the famous Edinburgh-to-London train, I brought up the subject of the landlord and his burgled safe for the first time since Holmes had refused to investigate. 'Holmes, were you not a little bit curt in refusing to help our host with his problem?'

He lowered his copy of *The Thunderer* and peered at me

irritably. 'My dear Watson, you promised me a holiday in Perthshire and, whilst fishing is hardly my pastime, I was quite enjoying the tranquillity of it all. During the last few days you have managed to involve me in a bizarre affair involving an eccentric illusionist, a man cremated in his stead and a series of missing bank deposit boxes. Not to mention the discovery of an eerie apartment that has not seen the light of day since the great plague. A clumsily-burgled village inn safe and a trifling sum lost would be too great an anti-climax, would it not? Next time you take me on a fishing holiday, please leave no word as to where we can be contacted!'